Sweet Wishes

Dana R. Lynn

AnniesFiction.com

Books in The Inn at Magnolia Harbor series

Library of Congress-in-Publication Data
Sweet Wishes / by Dana R. Lynn
p. cm.
I. Title
                    2020940589

AnniesFiction.com
(800) 282-6643
The Inn at Magnolia Harbor™
Series Creator: Shari Lohner
Editor: Lorie Jones
Cover Illustrator: Bonnie Leick

10 11 12 13 14 | Printed in China | 9 8 7 6 5 4 3 2 1

1

Grace

Grace Porter shook her head. This wasn't good. In fact, it was a disaster. A disaster she didn't have time to deal with.

She stared at the ATV tire tracks in the middle of the spacious and otherwise immaculate lawn of the Magnolia Harbor Inn, the bed-and-breakfast she owned with her younger sister, Charlotte Wylde. When Grace had gone to sleep the night before, the grounds had been perfectly groomed. Now they were a mess. A man-made mess. The tracks had destroyed the green landscape, with mud and uprooted flowers in every direction.

Neither she nor her sister owned an ATV. She mentally ran through the current guests at the inn. None of them had brought such a vehicle with them.

Grace regarded the large three-story antebellum mansion that was the heart of the Magnolia Harbor Inn. She and Charlotte had purchased it at auction many years ago. It had been a private residence, so they had remodeled and updated the interior.

The structure was more than just a building. Built in 1816, the mansion was part of South Carolina's history. Its previous owners included descendants of English aristocracy and French Huguenots. From the stately white columns to the wraparound porch, the building spoke of another era. Between the tastefully updated interior and the well-kept grounds, it was an ideal haven for those seeking a relaxing escape.

The sight of the ugly tracks against the pristine image of the mansion was almost painful for Grace. More than that, it was a deliberately hurtful act.

A yip at her feet distracted her from the destruction in front of her. Grace glanced down and smiled at Winston, her adorable little shih tzu mix, despite the ache in her heart.

Winston playfully stretched his forepaws out on the ground and wagged his tail. When he caught her gaze, he jumped up and pranced around her.

She laughed at his antics. Winston always brightened her day. He was a rescue dog, and she had fallen in love with him right away.

Winston fit right in at the inn. He loved greeting the new guests. He also seemed to possess the uncanny ability to sense when someone needed comfort or an extra snuggle. Grace couldn't imagine running the place without his sweet canine touch.

Reaching down, she ruffled his ears. When she straightened, she was once again met with the senseless vandalism.

Grace groaned, running her fingers through her shoulder-length dark-brown hair. She didn't need this stress. It was the beginning of August, the peak of their summer season, and they were booked solid for the rest of the month. The inn was hosting an anniversary party for Tim and Debby McFarland in only four days. The celebration would mostly take place outside on the lawn.

The same lawn that currently looked like it was under heavy construction.

Winston whined and gently touched his tiny paw to her shin.

"I'm okay, boy. Just a bit sad." *Not to mention anxious, angry, and utterly bewildered.*

This was not doing her any good. She needed to deal with the problem quickly instead of dwelling on it. Jesse McFarland, the couple's son, was scheduled to arrive later today. Grace hoped he wouldn't decide to cancel the event when he saw the mess.

Taking a deep breath, Grace closed her eyes and allowed the

honeysuckle-scented air to soothe her frayed nerves. The warm South Carolina sun pressed down upon her, its familiar warmth melting away some of her stress.

When Grace opened her eyes, the tension returned with a vengeance. What was she going to do? People came to the inn to find peace and healing. They wanted a respite from the problems of their everyday lives. How could they get that when a problem like this waited for them on the front lawn?

Angry again, Grace marched up the walkway and mounted the stairs, her heels clicking stridently on the wooden veranda. Winston's claws tapped on the wood at her side.

As she entered the mansion, she happened to glance down at her feet. On top of everything else, she'd gotten mud all over her new shoes. She grimaced when she noticed clumps of dirt scattered across the gleaming white ceramic tiles. Bending down, she slipped off the shoes and picked them up. She needed to clean her shoes and the floor before any of the guests arrived.

As she was straightening, Grace glimpsed something sticking out from underneath the table in the hall. She bent down and realized that it was an envelope.

"What's this?" Reaching out, she plucked the envelope up by the corner. It was no wonder she had missed it. It was a small cream-colored square, only four inches wide. The address was embossed on the front in gold lettering. It appeared to be an invitation. Obviously, she needed to return the envelope to the guest who had dropped it.

Turning the envelope over, she frowned. There was no return address. Grace tapped the envelope with one pink polished fingernail, thinking. The envelope was already stamped as well as sealed. It seemed logical to assume that whoever had dropped it intended to mail it. What should she do?

She placed the letter back on the table. Hopefully, the owner of the envelope would come searching for it and claim it.

Grace needed to contact Oliver Nichols, the owner of Two Green Thumbs, and ask him to assess the damage. Oliver's lawn care company did an impeccable job of maintaining the grounds at the inn. If anyone could fix this mess, it was him.

She also needed to contact Captain Keith Daley at the Magnolia Harbor Police Department—something that she dreaded doing. Not that she had a problem with the captain. He was an honest man and a fair and steady police officer. No, what she dreaded was having a police investigation, even a necessary one, disturb the peace her guests had come here to find.

There was no way around it, though. It had to be done.

She quickly made the necessary phone calls. The captain and Oliver both promised to stop by as soon as they could. After she hung up, she grabbed the cleaning supplies from the closet and tackled the dirty foyer, sweeping and scrubbing until the area was spotless.

As Grace returned the cleaning supplies to the closet, she heard the bell above the front door jingle and headed back to the foyer.

Winston dashed ahead of her, barking and wagging his tail.

When she entered the foyer, she saw the dog greeting a woman at the front desk. Two pieces of luggage were at her feet.

The woman was crouched down, petting Winston and cooing to him.

As usual, Winston didn't mind. In fact, he dropped to the floor and rolled over to give the woman access to his stomach. She grinned and rubbed his belly.

"I see you've met our welcoming committee," Grace said. "Winston loves making new friends."

The woman laughed, gave the dog a final pat, and stood. She was about two inches taller than Grace, and thick blonde curls fell to her shoulders. Everything about the new arrival screamed confidence—from her French manicure to her understated ice-blue pencil skirt and matching jacket. The summer heat was fierce, but she didn't seem to be bothered by it.

"Welcome to the Magnolia Harbor Inn," she said as she slipped behind the reception desk. "I'm Grace Porter, one of the owners."

"Nice to meet you." The woman smiled, her blue eyes sparkling. "I'm Olivia Pierce, and I have a reservation."

"Of course. We have you in the Buttercup Suite," Grace said as she handed Olivia a registration form and a pen. "It has a full view of Lake Haven, a king-size bed, a fireplace, and a private bath. We hope you'll enjoy it."

"It sounds wonderful." Olivia signed the form and returned it and the pen to Grace. "I can't wait to see it."

Grace filed the form, then grabbed the key. "I can show it to you whenever you're ready."

"Let's go," Olivia said as she picked up one of her bags.

Grace took the other bag and escorted Olivia to the second floor. Winston followed.

After unlocking the door to the suite, Grace stood back, allowing Olivia to enter. "Here it is."

"It's beautiful," Olivia gushed.

"I'm glad you like it." Grace smiled. She loved pleasing her guests. As she glanced around, she agreed with her guest's assessment of the elegant room with its yellow walls and gleaming hardwood floor. The dark wooden bed with its ornate headboard was the perfect match for the rose-patterned quilt, and the overstuffed armchair and ottoman near the fireplace provided a cozy nook.

"What an exquisite tub," Olivia said as she poked her head into the bathroom. "I'll definitely enjoy coming back here each evening after my business meetings."

"Excellent. I hope you'll join us this evening for hospitality hour. We serve hors d'oeuvres from six to seven on the back veranda. Breakfast is served in the dining room, and for dinner we encourage our guests to explore local restaurants."

"That sounds great," Olivia said.

"Please let me know if there's anything else you need," Grace said.

"Thank you."

Grace left Olivia to settle in. As she descended the stairs with Winston on her heels, she heard a vehicle pulling up. She peeked out the window and saw Oliver getting out of his Two Green Thumbs truck. Shoving a stray hair behind her ear, Grace strode outside to meet him.

Winston raced over to Oliver and wagged his tail.

"Hello, boy," Oliver said as he scratched behind the dog's ears.

"Thanks for coming so quickly," Grace said.

"No problem," Oliver said. "Now let's see what needs to be done."

For the next twenty minutes, Grace and Oliver walked around the yard. Winston trailed them, sniffing at the ground. Oliver detailed the list of repairs he and his crew would make and jotted down notes.

When they were done, Grace was afraid to ask, but she did anyway. "What do you think? Is it fixable?"

"Don't worry," Oliver said. "It seems bad now, but it's mostly surface damage. We'll take care of it."

She sighed in relief. It wasn't as bad as she had expected. Although it was bad enough. "We're hosting an anniversary party on Saturday. Will the yard be ready by then?"

Oliver nodded. "It'll be my highest priority. We'll have your lawn back in tip-top shape well before the anniversary party rolls around."

"That's great news. Thank you so much." Grace was glad that

she wouldn't have to call the McFarlands and tell him that their party needed to be canceled. She would have hated it, but it would have been the right thing to do. Hospitality was in Grace's very soul. Nothing brought her joy like helping others. Even if it meant losing their business, she couldn't let such a disaster ruin the couple's special day.

"I'll be in touch," Oliver promised. He returned to his truck and drove away.

As Grace headed to the front door, she heard another vehicle. She turned and saw Captain Daley parking his cruiser.

Daley emerged from the car and walked over.

Winston greeted the captain, then plopped down on the ground and stretched out.

"Thanks for stopping by," Grace said.

"I'm sorry this happened," Daley said, regarding the ruined yard. "Unfortunately, it's not surprising. This is the third call we've received for property destruction in the last few days."

"Oh no," she said. "What happened in the other places?"

"In all three cases, the vandals damaged property with historical significance to our area," he replied.

"How strange," Grace remarked.

Daley walked around the yard and took a few pictures. Winston trotted alertly beside him as if conducting his own investigation.

"Would you like a glass of sweet tea?" Grace asked when the captain was done.

"No thanks," he said. "I need to get going. I'll file a report and keep you informed."

"Thank you. I appreciate it."

He returned to his car.

Grace watched him leave and tried to control the frustration bubbling inside. It did no good to dwell on the situation. She had to trust the captain and Oliver to do their jobs, and she'd focus on doing hers.

Deliberately turning her back on the vandalized lawn, Grace walked to the porch and climbed the steps. She shivered. Knowing that someone was actively destroying property had taken some of the warmth from the day.

Winston padded to her side and followed her inside the inn.

In the foyer, Grace noticed that the envelope was still on the table where she'd left it. No one had come back for it yet. She picked up the envelope and frowned at it.

"Oh, there you are."

Startled, Grace glanced up. She'd been so preoccupied that she hadn't even heard Charlotte enter the room.

Grace smiled at her sister. She couldn't help herself. Charlotte was one of those people who radiated joy, and lately she had been especially happy. Grace knew it was partly because she was dating a man who complemented her so well. Charlotte and Dean Bradley, the owner of The Tidewater across the lake, had gotten off to a rocky start. Both were chefs, and there had been competition and some misunderstandings between them. But they had ironed out the misunderstandings, and the competition was healthy now. Currently, they were dating, and the relationship was going well.

Grace loved owning the inn with her sister. It had brought them closer together. Plus, it gave both of them the opportunity to use their gifts. One of Charlotte's gifts was that she was a fabulous cook. She had also written several best-selling cookbooks, and she'd recently landed a contract with a publisher who was as excited about her work as she was. Grace often marveled that Charlotte was content running the inn with her when she could own her own restaurant.

In her midthirties, Charlotte was as lovely and slim as any twenty-year-old, in spite of the long hours she spent baking and cooking delectable dishes for the guests.

Today Charlotte's blonde hair was pulled back into a low ponytail, and her dark-brown eyes were concerned. "What happened to the lawn?"

Charlotte lived in a small cottage on the property, so she would have seen the damage on her way to the inn. Her home was cozy with its combined bedroom and living room area, a bathroom, and a small kitchen. It had been built in 1835, and it had once been used as a chapel for the family and local villagers. Grace and Charlotte had redone the interior when they purchased the property.

"The police are investigating," Grace answered. "It seems there's been some vandalism in Magnolia Harbor lately."

"That's terrible," Charlotte said. "Did you call Oliver?"

"Yes. He stopped by a little while ago, and he's optimistic that he can fix the damage before the anniversary party."

Relief crossed Charlotte's face. Then she pointed to the envelope in Grace's hand. "What's that?"

Grace showed it to her. "I'm not sure. I found it under the table. It's been stamped already. There's no return address, so I don't know who it belongs to."

"You should go ahead and mail it," Charlotte said.

"Do you think so?" Grace asked.

Charlotte nodded, her ponytail bobbing. "Absolutely. It could be important. I'd hate for someone to miss a special event because their response got lost."

"You're right. Thanks." Grace added the envelope to the stack of outgoing mail. It was due to be collected soon.

Later that afternoon, Grace saw Becca Hart in the foyer, rifling through her black backpack. Becca was a young teacher, and she was working on her second master's degree. She'd told Grace that she came to the inn to work on her final project in a place where the rest of the world wouldn't intrude.

Grace approached her guest with a welcoming smile. "Is there anything I can assist you with?"

Becca whirled around, her eyes wide with panic. "I've misplaced something. A letter."

"Was it a small envelope?" Grace asked. "With gold writing on the front?"

Becca nodded, causing a few red curls to escape from her loose bun, but she didn't seem to notice. "Oh, I'm so relieved that you found it. You have no idea how worried I've been. I've searched everywhere."

Grace chuckled softly, glad that she was able to help. "Well, you can stop searching. I found it earlier. It was beneath the table in the foyer."

"Great," Becca said. She smiled and glanced around. "Where is it now?"

"Since it was already stamped and ready to go, I mailed it."

Becca's hopeful smile melted off her face, and an expression of absolute horror replaced it. She gasped. "Oh no!"

This was not the reaction Grace had expected. An uneasy feeling stirred in the pit of her stomach. "Weren't you planning on mailing it?"

"I changed my mind," Becca replied. "Oh, this is horrible. I'm in so much trouble!"

2

Becca

Becca Hart couldn't believe that Grace had mailed the envelope. What in the world was Becca going to do?

From Grace's distressed expression, the innkeeper felt awful about her part in Becca's situation. But it wasn't Grace's fault. She couldn't have known that Becca had only filled out the RSVP card in a fit of rage.

No, this whole situation was completely of Becca's own making. If she hadn't let her anger and sense of betrayal overrule her common sense, none of this would have happened. She grimaced. Well, she had. And now she had a disaster to deal with.

Winston, the sweet little dog she'd met when she first arrived, trotted over and whined at her.

Without thinking about it, Becca scooped up the dog, cradled him in her arms, and leaned her cheek against his soft head. He snuggled close to her, his soft little body a much-needed comfort.

"I'm so sorry," Grace said. "I should have waited to post the letter."

"No, it's fine," Becca lied, not wanting her gracious host to feel any worse.

Grace frowned slightly, clearly not believing her.

"Honestly, I'm sure everything will work out," Becca insisted.

"Please let me know if there's anything I can do to help," Grace said. "I feel responsible. Regardless of whether or not my actions have caused any problems, I regret not following my first instinct. If I can help you sort it out, all you have to do is ask."

Becca was touched. Earlier she had seen Grace outside with a police officer as he took pictures of the tire tracks and ruts in the yard. Obviously, the owners of the Magnolia Harbor Inn had their own issues to deal with. Yet here was one of them, sincerely offering her assistance without hesitation. It had been a long time since Becca had met anyone who acted out of simple kindness.

"Don't worry about it. I'll ask if I need something, but I'm sure it won't be necessary." Becca carefully set Winston on the floor. Even in her distress, her heart melted when he looked at her, his little tail wagging.

With a wave over her shoulder, Becca hurried upstairs to the Rosebud Suite on the second floor. Closing the door behind her, she crossed the room to the window and gazed out. Becca didn't even notice the breathtaking view of the garden below. All she could see was the sneer on her cousin Chelsea Hart's face when she received the RSVP card.

Groaning in frustration, Becca pressed her forehead against the cool glass. What had she been thinking? When she'd received the wedding invitation, she'd been angry and hurt beyond belief. But had she honestly ever planned on sending the RSVP to say she'd attend?

Becca pushed away from the window, then marched over to the gorgeous queen bed with its tall bedposts. She snatched the overly ornate invitation from the pristine white bedspread and reread it for the hundredth time.

Your presence is requested at the wedding of Chelsea Marie Hart and David Benjamin Walters.

The wedding was set for less than two weeks from now. David hadn't wasted any time at all. In fact, he must have been seeing Chelsea while he was still dating Becca. And Chelsea must have known it.

The rest of the text blurred. Becca tossed the invitation on the bed, then rubbed the tears off her face. Lately she'd cried enough to fill three rivers. She had believed she was getting over him, but this new betrayal had sent her running.

The moment she'd gotten the invitation in the mail, she'd packed her suitcase with enough clothes to last a month. She couldn't bear to deal with the looks of pity and the thinly veiled criticisms she was sure to get from her twin sisters. Victoria and Veronica were two years older than Becca. They had both married in the past year and had made no secret of the fact that getting Becca married was their shared goal in life. As if Becca needed the pressure.

And then there was Becca's mother. She was wonderful, but she was also a bit of a snob. When she had heard that David had broken off his engagement to Becca, she'd acted very offended. Becca had been stunned. Her own mother seemed more concerned about how her friends and relatives would react to her daughter losing a doctor than she was about Becca's broken heart.

Becca felt a stab of grief when she thought of her father. He'd passed away from heart disease three years ago. They had been close, and she'd always imagined him walking her down the aisle.

Leaving her home in Monroeville, Pennsylvania, for a few weeks had seemed like the perfect idea. Becca didn't have to worry about work. She taught first grade, and school didn't start until the last week in August. She'd miss the county fair, but it was okay. After all, she'd attended every year up until this point. Going to the fair for the twenty-fifth time didn't really seem that important when her whole world was imploding.

Becca had told her family that she was going away to work on her master's project. It was true, and she'd brought everything she needed with her. Then she'd searched online for a place to stay and had seen the Magnolia Harbor Inn. It had seemed ideal.

"My mistake was grabbing that stupid invitation before I left," she muttered. She still didn't know why she'd done it. She'd reached out and snagged it on her way out the door, then jammed it into her purse.

Now she picked it up again.

Chelsea. Her own cousin had stolen her fiancé. Until she'd read the invitation, she hadn't known that David and Chelsea were even dating. It all made sense now. Why he'd broken up with Becca so soon after she'd taken him to her family reunion. Why her traitorous cousin had stopped calling her. They'd always been close, but at the same time, they'd been rivals. For everything. Chelsea was the most competitive person Becca had ever met, and she always had to have the last word. But now her cousin had taken that competitiveness to a whole new level.

Becca would never forgive Chelsea for this.

Yesterday Becca had pulled the invitation out of her purse and had felt the petty need to prove to her former fiancé and her cousin that she was fine without either one of them. She'd rashly checked off that she'd be attending the wedding. With a guest. And then she'd written on the bottom of the card, *I can't wait for you to meet my new fiancé.*

Of course, it was a lie. Becca wasn't even dating anyone.

If only she'd paused to allow her better sense to kick in. Instead, she'd slipped the card into the envelope and sealed it. The defiance had worn off by that time. Chuckling bitterly, she'd shoved it into her purse before she left to go explore Magnolia Harbor. It must have fallen out as she was grabbing her keys from the purse while walking through the foyer. It was the only explanation.

Now it was too late to do anything. The envelope was in the mail. Within a couple of days, her mother and sisters would be calling Becca to ask who her fiancé was.

Chelsea would assume that Becca had been dating someone in secret. Why wouldn't she think that? During all the years the cousins had been competing and hanging out together, Becca had never told her a single lie. It wasn't who she was.

Except now she'd told the biggest whopper of them all.

Becca needed to get away from her thoughts. She slid her laptop and her binder of research notes into her backpack. Maybe she would go into town. She'd seen the Dragonfly Coffee Shop during her earlier visit. She could work there for a few hours and then grab a bite to eat before returning to the inn.

When Becca arrived downstairs, an older woman was at the reception desk. Her thick dark-blonde hair was lightly touched with gray and was pulled back into a neat bun.

"Good afternoon," the woman said with a smile. "You must be Becca Hart."

Becca nodded. She was immediately comforted by the warmth in the woman's smile. Her rich voice with its gentle Southern accent soothed Becca's wounded heart like a balm. "I was wondering if Grace or Charlotte was around."

"I'm Winnie Bennett, their aunt. Can I help you with something?"

Becca nodded. "I was planning to go to the Dragonfly Coffee Shop and work, and I was hoping to get a recommendation for a good restaurant for dinner."

"The Dragonfly is a great choice," Winnie said. "Josh Ford owns it, and I can personally vouch for the delightful atmosphere. As for dinner, I recommend Aunt Patsy's Porch. It's real home-cooked Southern food."

"It sounds good, but I'm diabetic," Becca said. "I need to watch my carbs and how much processed food I eat. Do they have some good choices for me?"

"I'm diabetic myself. Type 2." Winnie reached out and patted her hand. "Don't worry. I've never had a problem eating there. They have many tasty options."

"I think I'll check it out," Becca said.

Winnie jotted down directions on a piece of paper and handed it to Becca. "It's on I-95. You can't miss it."

"Thank you." Becca pulled the strap of her laptop case higher on her shoulder and headed to her car.

Soon Becca arrived in Magnolia Harbor. She slowed as she drove down the cobblestone street through the historic downtown district. It was lined with majestic old trees and quaint shops. She was charmed.

It didn't take her long to make it to the Dragonfly Coffee Shop. She found a parking space and turned off the engine, then grabbed her bag and opened the car door. As soon as she got out, the South Carolina heat hit her. Summers in Pennsylvania could get warm, but she wasn't used to this level of humidity. Her curly hair was going to frizz for sure. Frizzy red hair was not the look she wanted.

Shoving her glasses higher on her nose, she walked to the door and entered the cozy coffee shop. The heavenly aroma of coffee and pastries wafted in the air. A light strain of music played through the speakers. She might never want to leave this place.

Becca approached the counter.

"Welcome to the Dragonfly," the barista said with a smile. Her long dark hair was in a braid that hung down her back, and henna tattoos covered her hands. "Are you new in town or visiting?"

"I'm staying at the Magnolia Harbor Inn," Becca replied.

"It's a beautiful place. Charlotte and Grace are probably spoiling you rotten. They love to do that." The barista held out her hand. "I'm Angel Diaz."

"Becca Hart," she said as she shook Angel's hand. "Nice to meet you."

"I hope you enjoy your stay," Angel said. "Is there something I can get you?"

Becca scanned the menu board. "An unsweetened salted caramel tea, please."

"Great choice. Anything else?"

"Let me see." Becca peered at the display case and spotted fresh pain au chocolat. It had been years since she'd eaten the delicious French croissants filled with chocolate. She had checked her blood sugar before she left. One sweet treat wouldn't hurt. She had learned a long time ago that it was all right to indulge every now and then, as long as it didn't become a habit. "I'm going to be adventurous. I'll also have one pain au chocolat, *s'il vous plaît*."

"So you speak French?" Angel asked.

Becca winked. "Only what I remember from high school."

"Maybe you'll learn more while you're in the area," Angel said as she began preparing Becca's order.

"What do you mean?"

"Many people in Magnolia Harbor are of French descent," Angel explained.

"That's really interesting," Becca said. "I'll have to do some research about the town."

Angel set the tea and pastry on the counter. "Here you go."

"Thanks." Becca paid for her order, then took her laptop to a table in the corner and sat down. She opened the browser to the research articles she'd bookmarked earlier. The tea was good and hot, and the pastry melted in her mouth. The ambience in the coffee shop was perfect for encouraging creativity.

She read the first two paragraphs of the first article four times without making a single note. She couldn't even remember what she'd read. As much as she attempted to focus, thoughts of David and Chelsea kept intruding. What was Becca going to do? Obviously, she couldn't go to the wedding. But what was she supposed to say when people asked her about her fiancé?

She checked her watch. She'd been sitting here for nearly forty-five minutes and had accomplished nothing.

Pushing up her glasses with her index finger, Becca opened the second article and tried to concentrate. An hour later, she gave up. She'd made some progress but not nearly as much as she'd wanted to.

She slid her laptop into her bag and threw away her trash. As she headed toward the door, she waved at Angel.

"How was your croissant?" Angel called out.

"Incredible. Definitely a good decision."

Angel laughed. "Glad to hear it."

Becca wandered out onto the street with no idea where to go next. It was too early for dinner. Even if it wasn't, she knew anything she ate now would only sit in her stomach like a ball of lead.

Angel had been correct. The town was full of French influence. It was clear from some of the architecture. If Becca wasn't feeling so awful, she would have appreciated it a lot more. As it was, all she could think about was the fact that within twenty-four hours, she'd have to deal with the mortification of admitting that she had lied. People would understand. She was sure of that. As sure as she knew that many of them would forgive her out of pity.

Poor Becca. Dumped for her cousin.

What Becca would never understand was why no one ever seemed to fault Chelsea. Why didn't she have to suffer the consequences of her actions?

Becca frowned. She'd always been smarter and more athletic, but Chelsea had been the popular girl voted the most beautiful. While Becca brought home the grades, Chelsea had been the center of attention. And when she wasn't, she had done whatever was necessary to fix that.

Surely, though, Chelsea wasn't shallow enough to steal David away from Becca simply to prove that she could.

Was she?

Jesse

"Here we are—10 Lake Haven Road," the cabdriver announced, stopping the car in front of the Magnolia Harbor Inn.

Jesse McFarland slid his wallet from his back pocket and pulled out a credit card. He used the small credit card machine on the back of the driver's seat to pay the fare and added a tip.

"Thanks," the driver said, then popped the trunk.

Jesse exited the vehicle and hefted his duffel bag out of the trunk. After the cabdriver pulled away, Jesse turned to take his first look around the venue for his parents' thirty-fifth wedding anniversary party.

He wasn't impressed.

The inn itself was as gorgeous as all the pictures on the website had shown. He really liked the two-story wraparound veranda. What he didn't like were all the tire tracks in the lawn. What in the world had happened?

Jesse set his duffel bag on the ground. He took his cell phone out of his pocket and snapped a couple of pictures, then sent them to his siblings. Marlene and Zach weren't going to believe it. But it wasn't Jesse's fault. He had suggested renting a venue closer to home. Of course, they hadn't listened.

"Mom grew up near Magnolia Harbor," Zach had explained, as if Jesse didn't already know that. "She has family and old friends nearby. It's the perfect place."

Jesse had given in. Did it even matter what he thought? He'd been the black sheep of the family for as long as he could remember. In fact, it had been eight years since he'd gone home to New Albany, Ohio, to visit his parents.

After getting discharged, Jesse had moved into an apartment in Cleveland. When he'd called Zach out of the blue several weeks ago, his brother had given him a guilt trip. Their parents weren't getting any younger. Jesse had broken their hearts when he'd left without telling anyone where he was going. He was their baby, and their mother was worried about him.

The reality was that if Jesse hadn't gotten wounded while on his second tour of duty, he wasn't sure if he would have even come to see his family now.

Jesse had hung up the phone feeling two inches tall, and then his sister had called and given him the same lecture.

His phone rang, startling him out of his painful recollections.

"Is that what I think it is?" Zach demanded.

"It's nice to talk to you too."

"Hi," Zach snapped. "Seriously, what is that?"

"You know what it is. You can see the inn in the background. The yard is all torn up. I think they're ATV tracks."

There was a moment of silence. "What are we going to do? The party is this weekend."

The despair in Zach's voice struck a chord with Jesse. If he hadn't been here, if he hadn't finally decided it was time to reconnect, his family would be forced to deal with the situation alone. Jesse knew that his family was going through enough already. Marlene was recovering from chemotherapy. Her cancer was in remission, but her body had been weakened by the disease and the treatments. As for Zach, his accounting business was booming, and he was struggling to keep up with the demands.

Which was why Jesse had agreed to be the one to go to the inn a few days early and make sure everything was perfect.

"Don't sweat it," Jesse said. "It's too late to change the venue, as you've told me numerous times. But just in case, I'll ask about it. Maybe they'll have it taken care of before the party."

"That's optimistic," Zach said, "but I hope you're right."

"Maybe it won't be so bad," Jesse said. "I'm going to check in. I'll see what I can find out and text you later."

"Okay." His brother disconnected.

Jesse slid the phone into his pocket. Well, he couldn't stand out here all afternoon. He was tired after his long trip.

He slung his duffel bag over his shoulder and marched up the front steps, grimacing when he felt his knee twinge. He had a slight limp, and his healing limbs were protesting. As he entered the inn, a bell above the door jingled.

Jesse stopped to regard the impressive foyer. It was elegant but definitely not gaudy. He'd feared it would be. He liked things simple, but he could appreciate the tasteful decor.

A small dog trotted over. He wagged his tail while he sniffed Jesse's shoes.

Despite his fatigue and anxiety, Jesse smiled. He set his duffel bag on the floor and bent down to scratch behind the dog's ears.

The dog wagged his tail even faster.

He chuckled. "Hey, buddy. Nice to meet you too."

"Welcome to the Magnolia Harbor Inn," a blonde woman said as she entered the room. "I see you've met Winston. He loves to greet our guests."

"He's a nice dog," Jesse remarked.

"He really is." She smiled, her brown eyes sparkling. "I'm Charlotte Wylde, one of the owners. How may I help you?"

Jesse smiled in return. He judged her to be several years older than he was, but at twenty-five, he had learned to never try to figure out a woman's age. "I'm Jesse McFarland. I have a reservation."

Her smile dimmed slightly. "Please allow me to apologize for the state of our lawn. We were vandalized, but I assure you that we are already working to repair the damage."

"I'm sorry about what happened," Jesse said. "But I have to ask. Will we still be able to have my parents' anniversary party here?"

"Absolutely," Charlotte said. "The damage you saw outside is the only damage to the property. Our lawn care company has promised us that it can be taken care of well before the party on Saturday. It's their top priority."

"Well, let's hope for the best," he said.

"Thank you for understanding," Charlotte said. She went behind the registration desk. "Let's get you checked in."

"Sounds good," Jesse said, joining her at the desk. He needed a shower and food. Not necessarily in that order. He'd been unable to eat at the airport, and he hadn't stopped for a meal after he'd landed because he wanted to make it to the inn as soon as possible. It felt like he'd been traveling forever.

She retrieved a registration form and a pen, then handed them to Jesse.

As he reached out to sign the form, the wound on his left hand was clearly visible.

"I'm sorry about your injury," Charlotte said. "If you need any medication, we have most over-the-counter medications on hand."

"That's kind of you, but it isn't that bad." Jesse slid the signed form and pen across the desk. "I was injured in the military and discharged a few weeks ago. I have painkillers with me if I need them."

She blinked at him. Her eyes went glassy for an instant. "Thank you for your service."

Before he could respond, his stomach grumbled. Loudly. A wave of heat swept over his face.

Charlotte chuckled. "We don't usually provide lunch for our guests, but I could fix you something to tide you over until our hospitality hour at six o'clock. How about a club sandwich and homemade kettle chips?"

It was on the tip of his tongue to refuse, but then his stomach betrayed him with another grumble. "I'd appreciate it. I've been traveling all day."

"I'll be right back," Charlotte said, then hurried out of the room.

Winston kept Jesse company while he waited.

When Charlotte returned, she carried a tray with a sandwich, chips, and a bottle of water. She grabbed a set of keys at the desk. "Follow me. We'll get you settled."

As Jesse turned to pick up his duffel bag, he felt a stab of pain in his knee again, but he ignored it.

"You're in the Wisteria Loft Suite," Charlotte said, "but I'm afraid it's on the third floor. Would you like to move to a different room?"

"No, that's fine," Jesse said. He hadn't volunteered the information about his injury when he booked the room.

Charlotte ushered him to the suite. "It's the only room on this floor, so it's very private."

Jesse set his duffel bag on the trunk at the foot of the bed and glanced around. Like the foyer, the room was tastefully decorated. The king-size bed featured an ornate headboard, and the fireplace was flanked by two chairs.

"Let me know if you need anything else," Charlotte said. "Please join us on the veranda at six for hospitality hour. We'll have plenty of hors d'oeuvres and wine."

"Thank you," Jesse said.

After Charlotte left, Jesse munched on the sandwich and chips. From the French doors, he could see Lake Haven. As he gazed at the beautiful lake, the tension melted from his shoulders. The tranquil environment might be exactly what he needed to recover.

He polished off the rest of the sandwich, then flopped down on the soft bed. Maybe he would close his eyes for a minute.

4

Leslie

When Leslie Thomas arrived at the Magnolia Harbor Inn, she was exhausted.

A friend had recommended the inn to her a few months ago after spending a weekend here with her husband. At the time, Leslie couldn't imagine herself going to a bed-and-breakfast. She'd been too busy with her life as an heiress and socialite to think about a getaway. Not to mention the fact that she'd been dating the charming Will Canfield and the relationship was becoming more serious.

Until she'd discovered that Will was keeping horrible secrets from her.

A bell jingled as Leslie walked through the front door.

"Welcome to the Magnolia Harbor Inn," a dark-haired woman said as she entered the room. "I'm Grace Porter, one of the owners. How may I help you?"

Leslie enjoyed listening to the woman's South Carolina accent. It was so different than the crisp voices she was used to hearing in her hometown of Newark, New York.

Before Leslie could respond, a small dog bounded over to her, tail wagging.

"Oh, what a sweetheart." Leslie set her suitcase on the floor and knelt down so she could pet him. When he put his little paws on her knees and rose up as if to greet her, her heart melted.

"Winston loves making new friends," Grace said.

Leslie rubbed his soft fur with both hands. The urge to hug Winston was strong. "What kind of dog is he? I'll admit, I don't know much about the different breeds."

"He's a rescue dog," Grace answered. "We know he's part shih tzu, but the other part is a mystery."

Leslie gave him one final pat, then stood. "I don't have a reservation. This is an impromptu stop. My friend stayed here and bragged about the inn and the town, and I thought I'd see if you had any rooms available."

Plus, she doubted that Will would search for her in South Carolina.

Grace smiled. "You're in luck. We were booked solid, but this morning a guest called and canceled a room."

Leslie was so relieved she could cry. The mere idea of returning to her car and driving without a destination was enough to make her shudder. She'd already been traveling for more than a day. "Thank you. I'll take it."

"Let's get you checked into the Bluebell Suite," Grace said as she went behind the reception desk.

Leslie bit her lip. It wouldn't do to get too excited if she had to get back on the road tomorrow. Hopefully, she'd have a few days to make her plan. "How long is the room available?"

Grace turned to the computer and began clicking the keys. "It's available for the next two weeks."

So even if she needed a week or two, she wouldn't have to leave. "Perfect."

"The Bluebell Suite has a king-size bed and a partial view of Lake Haven," Grace said, handing Leslie a registration form and a pen. "You'll share a bathroom with the adjoining suite, but you have your own soaking tub in the room."

"It sounds wonderful," Leslie said. She didn't even mind sharing a bathroom. She signed the form and gave it to Grace.

"I'll show you to your room whenever you're ready," Grace said, filing the form.

Leslie picked up her suitcase. "I can't wait to see it."

Grace grabbed a key, and Winston led the way to the second floor.

When Grace opened the door to the suite, Leslie caught her breath. The room was exquisite with its robin's-egg blue walls, plush off-white furniture, cozy fireplace, and polished hardwood floor. Even the soaking tub added to the charm of the room. "I love it."

"I'm so glad," Grace said. She pointed to the French doors. "You can see Lake Haven from here."

Leslie walked over to take a peek. "It's lovely."

"Every evening from six to seven we have hospitality hour on the back veranda," Grace said. "I hope you'll join us. My sister, Charlotte Wylde, is an amazing chef, and she always prepares delicious appetizers."

"Sounds great."

"Breakfast is served in the dining room," Grace continued. "We don't provide dinner, but I can recommend a few local restaurants."

Leslie nodded. She wasn't concerned about dinner. She was so tired that she wasn't sure she would have enough energy to eat anyway. Besides, on the way she'd stopped at a travel plaza off the interstate and had devoured a rather robust chicken salad. The salad had been delicious, but it was the baguette that came with it that had caught her attention. It had still been warm, and she'd chewed it slowly to savor the rich flavor and dense texture.

"I'll let you settle in," Grace said. "Please let me know if you need anything."

"Thank you."

Grace and Winston left the room.

After they were gone, Leslie wandered around the suite. Then she grabbed a book from her bag and walked onto the veranda. It was warm, but she had expected it would be. Sinking down into one of the chairs, Leslie gazed at the lake for a moment without seeing it.

Had Will realized that she was gone? It was a good possibility, because he had a habit of showing up at her apartment unexpectedly. He'd called and texted her, but she hadn't answered or responded, and she didn't know whether she would. She'd considered blocking his number, but she decided that it was better knowing what his plans were.

Leslie didn't actually fear that Will would hurt her. He did have a bad temper, and she'd seen him explode and throw things. But his temper had never gotten away from him to the point that he'd hit her or—to her knowledge—anyone else.

At one time Leslie had believed that his intensity was romantic. As she had gotten to know him, it had kindled some unease in her, but she had no clue why that should be. It wasn't until last week when she'd overheard a phone call between him and a client that she realized the man she thought she was falling in love with didn't even exist. He'd been lying to her. Not only that, but he'd been using his relationship with her to cover his illegal actions.

Leslie had tried to pretend that she hadn't heard anything, but Will hadn't been fooled. He'd pierced her with a cold look she'd never forget.

Shivering, she shook her head to dislodge the disturbing memories. Chances were very slim that Will would search for her here. If he bothered to search for her at all.

Although there was always the chance that he would want to find her to make sure she wouldn't go to the police and turn him in.

No, Leslie would not dwell on it. What was done was done, and there was nothing she could do to change it now. She was staying in the most peaceful place she'd ever visited, and she would enjoy it. Will would never find her here.

Determined to stop thinking about her ex-boyfriend, she opened her book and started reading. It was an old favorite that always soothed her, and she soon drifted off to sleep.

Sometime later Leslie awoke to the sound of a dog barking. Beyond the veranda, she glimpsed Winston catching a ball, then running back to Grace. Standing beside Grace was a younger blonde woman.

Grace threw the ball again. "Go get it, Winston!"

The little bundle of fur barked once, then chased the ball.

Leslie laughed softly. Winston was adorable. "When all this is over and I have my life back, I'll get a dog."

It was one more item on a long list of things she'd do someday.

Right now, though, she needed to concentrate on living day to day.

Standing, she closed her book and returned to the room. Now that she was awake, she regretted not eating anything. She'd have to go downstairs for hospitality hour.

Leslie felt a bit rumpled from her nap. She'd feel more like herself if she freshened up. Grabbing her toiletry bag, she headed to the bathroom to wash her face and brush her teeth. The door was closed, so she knocked.

A young woman with red hair opened the door. "You must be my bathroom mate." She smiled. "I'm Becca Hart."

"Leslie Thomas. I haven't had a shared bathroom since college. It brings back memories."

They chatted for another moment before Becca excused herself.

Leslie hurried to get ready, but she couldn't stop worrying about Will. Uneasiness took root in her heart, and she feared that he would find her, no matter how firmly she tried to dismiss the idea.

Would she ever feel safe again?

5

Jesse

When Jesse opened his eyes, it was nearly five thirty in the evening. He laughed to himself. Obviously, he had needed the sleep.

Jesse was wide awake now. He didn't feel like going into town, and he didn't want to stay in his room with only his gloomy thoughts for company. Charlotte had said hospitality hour was at six. If he showered quickly, he could make it in time. Maybe he'd find someone to talk to. Anything to take his mind off his parents' anniversary party and the regrets of his past.

Decision made, he headed to the shower. He kept it short, although he would have liked to linger.

Once Jesse was dressed in blue jeans and a T-shirt, he went downstairs to meet the other guests. There was an even better view of the lake on the back veranda. He got in line at the buffet table.

The older man in front of him turned and held out his hand. "Gus Bennett. Nice to meet you."

"Jesse McFarland," he said as he shook it. "Have you ever stayed here before?"

Gus laughed. "Yes, although I'm not what you'd call a guest. Grace and Charlotte, who own the inn, are my nieces by marriage. My wife, Winnie, and I don't live far from here."

"I met Charlotte," Jesse told him. "She made me a sandwich."

"Then you're a lucky man," Gus said, with more than a hint of paternal pride. "Our Charlotte is an accomplished chef. She's responsible for all this delicious food."

Jesse scanned the buffet table covered with tantalizing appetizers. The sandwich he'd eaten had been delicious, but it hadn't quite satisfied his hunger. He grabbed a plate and filled it, then scanned the veranda to choose a spot to sit before he moved. It was easier to walk as little as possible on days when his leg was sore.

There was an empty seat at one of the tables next to an adorable younger woman with curly red hair. A pair of glasses with greenish-blue frames sat on her pert nose, and she was reading a book. It was her expression that caught his attention, though. Even as she smiled at something she was reading, her face seemed to hold a deep sadness. Then the expression was gone. He knew he hadn't imagined that look. It intrigued him. He felt as if he'd been gifted with a glance of a kindred spirit.

Jesse approached the table and pointed at the empty chair. "Is anyone sitting here?"

The redhead glanced up at him, obviously startled. "Help yourself."

"Thanks." He sat down and set his plate on the table.

The woman returned to reading her book.

"I'm Corporal Jesse McFarland." He cringed as soon as the words left his mouth. Why had he added his rank? He wasn't in the Army anymore. "Let me correct myself. I *was* a corporal. Now I'm only a civilian." He cringed again. "Sorry. I'll stop talking now."

She grinned. "That's okay. Sometimes I say things without thinking too." A shadow passed over her face. "I've even been known to write things without thinking." She shook her head. "Anyway, I'm Becca Hart."

"What brings you to Magnolia Harbor?" Jesse asked, then took a bite of a meatball dipped in sweet-and-sour sauce. It was tasty. "I'm here for my parents' anniversary party."

Becca hesitated. "I'm working on my master's project."

That wasn't the whole story. He could tell there was more. However, who was he to judge or ask her to share more than she wished? "Cool. May I ask what your project's on?"

Her entire face lit up.

His breath caught in his throat. He had been wrong. She wasn't merely adorable. When she smiled like that, she was radiant.

Becca launched into a description of her thesis. Most of it dealt with teaching the subject of reading and educational practices.

"Are you a teacher?" he asked.

"First grade," she said. "This will be my third year."

Jesse chuckled. "You're brave. I think a roomful of six-year-old kids would be intimidating."

"No, the kids are great," Becca said. "They're so eager to learn. Well, at least most of them. For those who aren't, you only have to figure out how to make learning exciting for them, and that's fun."

Charlotte and a dark-haired woman came over to the table and greeted Jesse and Becca.

"I wanted to introduce you to my sister, Grace Porter," Charlotte said to Jesse. "We own the inn together."

Mindful of his manners, Jesse stood to shake her hand. "Good to meet you."

"And you," Grace said. "I want you to know that we're doing everything we can to ensure that the grounds will be perfect for your parents' anniversary party."

"Glad to hear it," Jesse responded. "I know they'd be mighty disappointed if we had to move the event."

They talked about last-minute party arrangements for a few minutes, and then the owners moved on to greet their other guests.

Jesse caught the expression on Becca's face. The sadness was back in her eyes. What was that about? "Do you—"

"It's been nice talking to you," Becca said, cutting him off. "I'm really tired, and I need to go back to my room. I'm sorry." She stood and scurried away.

Jesse stared after her. He had no idea what had happened. It was probably just as well. Becca was obviously a bright woman with ambitions. A woman who had a vision of who she was and where she was going.

What did he have to offer someone like that? He was an ex-soldier who'd disappointed his family more often than not. Right now, he was a man without a plan for his future.

Becca Hart was way out of his league. The best he could do for her was to stay out of her life.

6

Leslie

It was going on six when Leslie left her room. As she headed to the veranda, she spotted Becca rushing toward the stairs. She was obviously upset.

"Are you all right?" Leslie asked.

Becca stopped and wiped her eyes. "Yes, I'm fine. Just tired." She hurried away.

Leslie was concerned, but she didn't want to intrude, so she continued to the veranda.

Grace greeted her warmly. "I'm glad you could join us. Let me introduce you to the other guests." She led Leslie to a table and gestured to a young man. "This is Jesse McFarland. He's here for his parents' anniversary party this weekend."

Leslie shook his hand. "Nice to meet you." Judging by his short hair and the manner in which he held himself, she guessed he was in the military.

"This is Olivia Pierce," Grace said, motioning to a lovely blonde woman. "She's here on business."

"Nice to meet you too," Leslie said.

"And Joseph and Marge Alton are passing through," Grace said.

Leslie greeted the older couple.

"We live in Jacksonville, and we're on our way to see our daughter and son-in-law in Charlotte." Marge smiled. "They're expecting a baby in two weeks."

"Congratulations," Leslie said.

"We left early so we could spend some time here," Marge said. "It's a charming town. If you're here for a while, make sure you check out the shops downtown."

"I'll make that a priority for sure," Leslie replied.

Grace ushered Leslie over to the buffet table. "Please enjoy."

Leslie selected a cannoli and a variety of vegetables and stuffed mushrooms. She drizzled dressing over the vegetables and helped herself to a cup of coffee. There was an empty seat, somewhat isolated, near the end of the veranda, and she walked over to it.

Even sitting by herself, it was a restful environment. She breathed deeply, inhaling the sweet scent of flowers from the vase on the table.

Leslie took a small bite of the cannoli. Her eyes widened as an explosion of sweetness tingled on her taste buds.

"Delicious, aren't they?" a soft voice murmured.

Leslie turned and saw an older woman standing beside her. "Amazing."

"My niece Charlotte made them."

"If this is only one example of her cooking, then I'm really looking forward to tasting more," Leslie remarked.

"Charlotte's a terrific cook. She used to be the head chef at an upscale restaurant in Charleston, and she's written a few best-selling cookbooks."

"That's impressive," Leslie said.

The woman sat down across from her. "I'm Winnie Bennett."

"Good to meet you. I'm Leslie Thomas."

"My husband, Gus, and I live nearby," Winnie said. "I stop by often to see my nieces and lend a hand, so I'm sure we'll be seeing each other during your stay."

Leslie immediately liked Winnie. She was confident yet gentle—a compelling mixture. "I don't know how long I'll be here. I left a bad situation at home. The man I thought I'd spend my life with turned out to be involved in something terrible. I don't know all the details, but he's been taking bribes. I was confused, so I ran." She shook her head. Why was she sharing such intimate details with a stranger?

Winnie leaned closer. "Did you go to the police?"

The mere idea of going to the police made her shudder. "No. I'm not sure that anyone would believe me."

"Why not?"

"Will has friends in high places," Leslie said. "He's on the city council and is running for mayor. I figured that I needed some time to get my thoughts in order before I do anything."

"You came to the right place," Winnie assured her. "I can think of no better atmosphere to soothe your soul and untangle your troubles to help you make the right decisions."

It was an odd way to phrase it, but the words settled into her soul and made sense. Her world was a tangled mess right now, and she needed to unwind the threads to find the right path.

Winnie gestured to the entrance. "There's Charlotte. I'm sure she would love to meet you." She waved her niece over.

Charlotte joined them.

"Have you met Leslie Thomas?" Winnie asked her niece.

"Not yet," Charlotte said, then turned to Leslie. "We're so glad you're staying with us. Please let us know if you need anything."

Leslie smiled at her. "Thank you."

"Leslie and I have been talking about you," Winnie told Charlotte.

"Really?" Charlotte asked, raising her eyebrows.

Winnie grinned. "Well, we've been talking about your wonderful cooking."

"I'm so happy to hear it," Charlotte said. "I do love to cook."

"It shows," Leslie said.

"And I was telling Leslie about your cookbooks," Winnie added.

"Winnie might be my biggest fan," Charlotte said to Leslie in a confidential tone. "She always acts as if everything I do is the best thing since sliced bread."

"I'm usually right," Winnie replied loftily.

"If your cookbooks feature more food like this," Leslie said, holding up the cannoli, "I'm inclined to believe her."

"I'm working on a new one," Charlotte said, "so you might get to sample some of my new recipes while you're staying with us. Feedback is crucial to making a new recipe successful."

"That would be great," Leslie said.

"Excuse me, girls," Winnie said. "I need to talk with Grace before I return home." She gave Charlotte a hug, then walked away.

Charlotte sat down in the chair that Winnie had vacated. "Do you cook?"

"No," Leslie admitted. "Although food has always been a passion of mine. I love to watch cooking shows on TV. That probably seems weird, especially since I never actually make the food. I have so many cookbooks that I've never used. I would love to learn, but until now, I've never had the time. Or at least that's the excuse I've always given. In truth, I'm not sure where to begin . . ." She let her words fade as she realized she'd been babbling.

"I understand," Charlotte said. "I should greet the other guests, but if you're not busy, maybe we could talk more about cooking after breakfast tomorrow morning. I love sharing what I know. Maybe I can help point you in the right direction."

Leslie agreed immediately, hope and excitement rising inside her.

After Charlotte left, Leslie finished her appetizers and then made her way to her room.

She sat in front of the fireplace and prayed for clearer vision.

One thing was certain. No matter what happened, Leslie was determined that she'd rely on herself from now on. A man would have to be more than charming and well connected to get her trust or her heart.

He'd have to prove that he had integrity and was worth her time.

7

Leslie

Leslie couldn't remember the last time she'd slept in past six o'clock in the morning. She was more exhausted than she'd thought. Her grumbling stomach made her aware of how little she'd eaten yesterday. It was not the day to skip breakfast, especially after tasting the delicacies offered by the inn last evening.

Charlotte was going to meet with her later this morning about cooking. Sudden excitement chased away any remaining sleepiness. She couldn't wait to pick the brilliant chef's brain.

Shoving back the covers, Leslie rushed through her shower and morning routine. Instead of the full makeup she would normally wear, she cleaned and moisturized her face and put on mascara and a coral lipstick. She brushed her short blonde hair and added hair spray to keep it in place.

Leslie dressed in a green short-sleeved shirt and a pair of khakis. A simple pair of gold hoop earrings completed her outfit.

She had never gotten ready so quickly. Usually, she spent at least thirty minutes on her face and hair. Today she'd finished in five.

After grabbing her purse, Leslie left her suite and went downstairs to the dining room. It was empty.

For a moment, she regarded the room. There was an understated elegance in the large dark-wood table and the classic white cushioned chairs spread evenly around it. The ceiling was high, and light streamed in through the large window at the far end of the room. She rounded the table and peered out the window. She had a clear view of Lake

Haven. The blue water sparkled in the warm summer sun. It was a view that she would love to see every day.

When Leslie heard voices behind her, she turned.

Becca entered the room with Jesse. He was smiling at Becca as if he were completely enchanted.

When I meet the man I'll marry, I want him to smile at me like that, Leslie thought.

"Good morning," Becca said to Leslie.

"Nice to see you both again," Leslie responded.

"When did you two meet?" Becca asked.

"At hospitality hour last night," Jesse answered. He turned to Leslie. "I didn't get a chance to ask if you're here for business or if you're on vacation."

Leslie hesitated, wondering how to respond. "It's kind of a vacation."

Fortunately, Jesse wasn't able to ask her any more questions about what she was doing in Magnolia Harbor because Grace and Charlotte walked in with trays of food.

"We're sorry to keep you waiting," Grace said, putting a tray of fresh fruit on the buffet table. She motioned to the carafes. "We have coffee and orange juice."

"Please help yourselves." Charlotte set trays of omelets, bacon, and sausage on the table.

"Good morning, everyone," Olivia said as she breezed into the room.

Joseph and Marge were the last ones to arrive.

The guests filled their plates, then sat down at the table. Grace and Charlotte joined the group, and they all made small talk.

"Where are you going today?" Grace asked the Altons.

"Prescott Park," Joseph answered.

"I can't wait to see the Prescott Pottery factory ruins," Marge added.

"It's a beautiful place," Charlotte said. "If you're interested in art, you should also check out the Dorothy A. Prescott Arts Center in downtown Magnolia Harbor."

"We'll add it to the list," Joseph said.

While the guests chatted, Leslie savored the delicious food and returned to the table for seconds.

As breakfast was winding down, Becca turned to Leslie. "I might go into town later. You're welcome to come with me."

Leslie appreciated the gracious invitation, but she felt like sticking close to the inn today. "Thanks, but I have some things to do on my own today. Have a good time."

"You too," Becca said with a smile.

The other guests gradually filed out of the room, but Leslie remained where she was. There was no way she was going to miss the opportunity to talk with Charlotte again.

"Do you still have time to chat?" Charlotte asked.

"Yes, and I'm looking forward to it," Leslie said.

"Me too," Charlotte said. "I'll be back in a few minutes after we clean up."

Grace and Charlotte quickly cleared the table and disappeared into the kitchen.

A few minutes later, Charlotte returned with two steaming mugs of coffee and slid one to Leslie as she took a seat. "My sister insisted that I take a break from breakfast dishes and let her handle them. She knows how much I love to talk about cooking." She took a sip from her mug. "So, where are you from?"

"Newark, New York." Leslie wondered how much she should say, then decided to plunge ahead. "I have no family left. My parents were both killed in a car accident two months after I graduated from college, and I'm an only child. There's nothing holding me there."

She'd never allowed herself to consider that before. There really was nothing in New York that she wouldn't be willing to leave. She could literally go anywhere and start over. The possibilities seemed endless. Leslie wasn't hurting for money. Her parents had left her a small fortune. And without having a spouse, children, or pets, she could completely rebuild her life to fit her own desires.

"I'm so sorry that you lost your parents," Charlotte said. "I know how devastating it is."

Charlotte told Leslie about losing her father to a heart attack and her mother to complications from pneumonia. They talked about their families for a few minutes, and then the conversation shifted to cooking.

"I don't know how to cook, but I've always wanted to learn," Leslie admitted. "When I was growing up, my parents hired a cook, and I wasn't allowed to bother her in the kitchen. During college, I survived by ordering out and eating microwavable meals."

"Do you cook any of the basics now?" Charlotte asked.

"I can whip up a grilled cheese sandwich when absolutely necessary, but that's about as far as my culinary skills go."

"It sounds like you should invest in a beginner cooking class first," Charlotte advised. "If you decide you like it, you could take classes that specialize in more advanced techniques."

"That's a great idea," Leslie said. "Maybe if things go well after that I could eventually go to culinary school."

Charlotte nodded. "There are many culinary programs to choose from. A lot of them focus on the technical aspect, but some also focus on restaurant management or hospitality. You could do some research to find out what kinds of programs are out there and what interests you."

Leaning back in her chair, Leslie sighed. "I'd hate to invest in a class only to find out that I hated it or wasn't any good."

"Are you busy now?" Charlotte asked.

"No. Why do you ask?"

"I'm going to give you a cooking lesson." Charlotte stood.

"Really?" Leslie asked as she shot out of her chair. "I'd love that. But do you have time?"

Charlotte laughed. "I always have time to cook."

"Thank you so much," Leslie said. "You don't know what this means to me."

"It's my pleasure." Charlotte led the way into the spacious kitchen and showed Leslie around. She described the various appliances and utensils and how they were used. She also explained cooking rules and health standards.

After Charlotte covered the basics, she talked about recipes. "You can find great recipes online, of course, but sometimes there's nothing like a good old cookbook." She removed a thick one from a shelf. "It won't time out on you, and you don't need to worry about spilling flour or oil on the screen."

"Good point," Leslie remarked.

"Would you like to choose a recipe?" Charlotte asked, handing the cookbook to Leslie.

"I already know what I want to do first," Leslie answered. "I want to try my hand at making cannoli."

"Those are always fun," Charlotte agreed. "It will take us nearly two hours to make them. Would that work for you?"

"Absolutely," Leslie said. "Are you sure you don't mind spending that much time with me?"

"I have to cook for hospitality hour this evening anyway, so it'll be fine," Charlotte said. "While the cannoli are chilling, we'll start on another dish." She ran her finger down the list of ingredients. "We have everything we need to make them."

Charlotte moved smoothly around the kitchen, collecting the ingredients. "I always gather everything I need before I begin. That way there are no surprises, such as realizing that you're out of cinnamon after you've already mixed the dough for snickerdoodles."

Leslie chuckled. "I can see myself doing something like that."

The kitchen was a flurry of activity as the women made cannoli, avocado dip for fresh vegetables, prosciutto rolls, bacon-wrapped dates with almonds, ricotta crostini with chestnut honey, and finally chocolate cupcakes with caramel ganache and coconut.

Leslie followed Charlotte's directions to the letter and frequently asked questions. Charlotte was a patient teacher, always taking the time to demonstrate the correct procedure before Leslie attempted it. As they worked, Leslie's enthusiasm and confidence grew.

"This is wonderful," Leslie remarked, wiping down the counter. "I never realized how much joy cooking could bring."

"It can. And I will tell you that you have a natural gift for it. You followed the directions precisely, and your questions were completely on point."

In that moment, a dream was born in Leslie's mind. "I know it sounds crazy, but this is what I want to do. I'm not sure what shape it will take—whether I'll become a chef somewhere or open my own restaurant—but I want a career in cooking."

She felt the rightness of the words and knew she'd found her calling. It would definitely take some deeper thought to flesh out which career path she'd focus on, but she finally had a direction to go in.

For the first time in her life, Leslie had an ambition that didn't rely on her parents' money or a boyfriend's approval.

It felt wonderful.

Grace

Judging by the laughter coming from the kitchen, Charlotte and Leslie were having a grand time. And from the tantalizing aromas wafting through the air, the guests would be in for a treat at hospitality hour this evening.

Grace smiled contentedly. There was nothing that gave her more pleasure than knowing that her guests were happy and enjoying their time away from the stress of their everyday lives. She was especially pleased by how relaxed Leslie appeared. It had been obvious when she saw the young woman at breakfast that her smiles were forced. Charlotte was very good at spreading joy and encouraging people to open up. It was one of her gifts.

As Grace walked to the reception desk to check for messages, Joseph and Marge rushed downstairs with their luggage.

"Is something wrong?" Grace asked, alarmed.

"Our daughter went into labor," Marge said. "We need to get to Charlotte as soon as possible."

"We're sorry for checking out early," Joseph said.

"It's not a problem," Grace said. "The important thing is for you to be with your family and meet your new grandchild."

"Thanks for understanding," Marge said. "We appreciate it."

After Grace checked them out, the couple said goodbye and hurried out the door.

Grace checked the messages, then stopped by the kitchen to tell Charlotte that the Altons had checked out early.

Then she glanced out the window and decided to do some gardening. She went to her private quarters and changed into a T-shirt, shorts, and tennis shoes.

Winston trotted over to her.

"Would you like to join me outside?" she asked.

The dog dashed to the door and glanced over his shoulder at her. She laughed. "Let's go."

Grace grabbed her supplies and headed to the garden with Winston. He kept her company as she worked the soil and pulled weeds. Spending time outdoors in the sunshine always relaxed her.

When her work was done, she gathered her supplies and turned to Winston. The dog was trotting between bushes, sniffing the ground. "Ready to go inside?"

Winston's head came up, and he yipped.

When they entered the inn, Grace wiped the dirt off Winston's paws, then washed her hands.

The phone rang, and she hurried to answer it.

It was Oliver. "I'm getting ready to come over to the inn," he said. "The crew is going to start the repairs this morning."

"Thank you," Grace said. She couldn't wait to tell Jesse that the project was moving forward. He had been gracious when she'd explained the situation, but it was apparent that the state of the lawn was a huge concern to him. It was for her and Charlotte too.

"We'll be over in fifteen minutes," Oliver said.

"Fifteen minutes?" Grace repeated. She glanced down at her gardening clothes. It wouldn't be enough time to shower and change, but that couldn't be helped. If all went well, she could greet the workers and then slip away to make herself presentable before anyone else saw her. Grace wasn't vain, but she was always conscious of the image she projected as the owner of the inn.

"Is that a problem?" Oliver asked.

"No, it's fine," Grace assured him. She couldn't afford for it not to work. There was too much to do to take care of the inn and prepare for the anniversary party. "I'll see you then." She disconnected.

"Come on, Winston. We have to get ready. Quickly." Grace strode to her private quarters with Winston on her heels.

As Winston made a beeline for his dog bed, she straightened her appearance as much as possible. She combed her hair and piled it into a messy bun. At least she didn't have dirt smudged on her nose.

"What do you think?" she asked Winston.

He jumped out of his bed and wagged his tail.

She laughed. "I can always count on you to be supportive." She checked the clock. "Let's go wait for Oliver and his crew on the porch."

They headed to the front door. When she opened it, she saw Spencer Lewis climbing the porch stairs.

Spencer was their neighbor and a good friend. A little over fifty, he was tall and fit. Not to mention handsome with his light-blue eyes, salt-and-pepper hair, and easy smile. At one point, she'd considered a deeper relationship with him.

Neither of them had had an easy path in the area of romance. Spencer's wife had died of breast cancer almost a decade ago. Grace had thought her husband, Hank, had passed away in a train accident in Prague over twenty years before. She'd raised their son, Jake, alone. After Jake had moved to Raleigh, North Carolina, Grace had been ready to move on.

Until Hank had suddenly returned a few months ago. He'd left her so he could build a life without a wife and child, then decided he wanted his family back all those years later. Grace and Jake had both been uncomfortable with it even before they had discovered that he'd been involved in highly illegal activities. It had almost been a relief when he was arrested. He was no longer part of either of their lives.

Unfortunately, Hank's appearance had left her exhausted and emotionally drained. She'd told Spencer that she needed some time to come to terms with Hank's betrayal and all that had happened. Spencer had seemed disappointed, but he had been gracious and understanding.

"Good morning," Grace said, brushing a strand of hair off her forehead. "What a pleasant surprise."

"I was in town running errands," Spencer said as he walked inside, "and I heard about the vandalism. I wanted to see how you were doing."

Winston ran around Spencer in circles.

"I'm sorry this happened," Spencer said, reaching down to pet the dog. "I would have come over yesterday if I'd known."

His usual calm demeanor made Grace relax. Spencer was a retired intelligence analyst for the FBI, and she had no trouble imagining him in that demanding position. He was smart and reliable, and he easily and serenely handled any surprises that were thrown his way.

Grace wished she possessed a similar ability. Life's curves had sent her reeling more than once, and it had taken her a long time to regain her equilibrium.

"I know you would have, and I appreciate it," Grace said. "I thought about calling you, but I didn't want to bother you."

"You wouldn't have been bothering me," Spencer said. "I would have come to support you."

Grace realized that he was hurt. She rested her hand on his arm. "I'm sorry. I didn't think about that. I was—"

"Spencer Lewis!" someone called out.

Grace jumped as Olivia hurtled toward them. Winston skittered over to Grace's side. She was surprised by her dog's reaction because he usually loved cuddling up to guests.

Olivia threw her arms around Spencer and hugged him. His head was momentarily obscured behind her big blonde hair.

Any amusement Grace might have felt was overshadowed by the hollow feeling growing in the pit of her stomach.

Olivia wore a flowing blue-and-white floral sundress with spaghetti straps and gold sandals. She appeared fresh and pretty.

Unlike herself. Grace glanced down at her own attire. Although she'd cleaned up, she still wasn't looking her best in a T-shirt, shorts, and tennis shoes. Plus, her hair was an absolute disaster. She resisted the urge to try to fix her messy bun. It was what it was. She wasn't trying to impress anyone.

Spencer laughed and hugged Olivia briefly, then stepped back. He held her at arm's length and smiled, his eyes crinkling at the corners. "I didn't know you were here."

"I'm in town on extended business," Olivia said.

"Oh?" Spencer raised his eyebrows. "What kind of business?"

Olivia flashed him a blinding smile. "I'm a marketing specialist for a large real estate developer in Austin, Texas. My company has a project in the area that I'm assisting with."

Spencer whistled. "Impressive. You've done well. How long will you be around?"

"I'm not sure." Olivia shrugged. "I thought it was going to be dull staying in a small town."

Grace gritted her teeth behind her smile. Magnolia Harbor might be a small town, but it certainly was not dull.

"Dull?" Spencer asked, echoing Grace's disbelief. "I'm surprised to hear you say that. You always loved historic places."

"I know. I guess I've gotten used to life in a big city," Olivia said. "What are you doing here?"

"I live nearby," Spencer answered. "On a small pecan farm."

Olivia grinned. "Now that I know you're here, my outlook of the place has definitely improved."

Spencer glanced at Grace. "I'm sorry. I don't mean to be rude and exclude you from the conversation. Olivia and I have known each other for a long time. We met at Baylor years ago."

Olivia laughed. "*Oui*, we met in French class. But you're forgetting something, Spencer. We didn't just go to school together. We dated for two years. In fact, we were inseparable at one time."

He cleared his throat and shifted, then glanced at Grace again.

Grace wondered if he was embarrassed.

"How have you been?" Spencer asked Olivia, obviously changing the subject. "I heard you were married."

"I'm divorced now, and I have two grown sons," Olivia said. "What about you? Did you get married?"

"I'm a widower," Spencer said. "Nearly ten years now."

"My, that's a long time to be alone," Olivia said, batting her eyelashes at him.

Grace felt the juvenile urge to roll her eyes. She had never actually seen anyone bat their lashes. It was a ridiculous affectation.

Immediately, shame swept through her. Olivia was a lovely woman talking to a former boyfriend. She was also a guest at the inn. Grace had no reason to harbor any negative feelings against her. Even if she was jealous.

No, Grace wasn't jealous. She was absolutely fine remaining friends with Spencer. Besides, she was the one who had insisted on it. Which meant he was free to date other women.

But she still didn't like it.

The conversation was interrupted when Oliver and his small lawn care crew arrived.

"I'd better go and let them work," Spencer said.

"It was fantastic to see you," Olivia said. "We need to get together while I'm in town."

"That sounds great," Spencer said.

Olivia took her phone out of her purse. "What's your number?"

After they exchanged phone numbers, Spencer said, "I'll be in touch."

"Thanks for stopping by," Grace told him.

"I'll talk to you later," he said. "Call if you need me."

"I will," Grace promised.

Spencer said goodbye to the women, then walked out the door.

"Oh, this is wonderful," Olivia said. "I haven't seen Spencer in so long. I always wondered what had become of him. And we're both single again. Wouldn't it be something if we reconnected while I'm here?"

"Yes, it certainly would." Grace was itching to escape the outgoing woman's chatter. "Please excuse me. I need to talk with the lawn care crew about the work they'll be doing."

"Of course. I have to get to a meeting anyway." With a wave, Olivia left.

Grace rubbed her temples, then went outside with Winston following.

Oliver exited his truck and approached Grace with a small container. Winston bounded over to greet him.

Oliver petted the dog, then gave Grace the container. "I told Elaina about the vandalism," he said, referring to his wife and the receptionist of Two Green Thumbs. "She insisted on making you a batch of her grandmother's chocolate-covered cherry cookies."

"She didn't have to do that," Grace said, accepting the container. "However, I'll never turn down her delicious cookies. Please tell her thank you."

"I will." Oliver adjusted his sunglasses. "Now let's see what we can do about your lawn."

"I can't tell you how much I appreciate you and your workers making this a priority," Grace said.

"We're all friends here," Oliver said. "You know that. That's what friends do. Besides, I know that if Elaina and I ever needed help, you, Charlotte, and Winnie would be the first people at our door."

Grace smiled. "Thanks again."

Oliver called his crew together, and they began removing their equipment from the trucks.

Grace and Winston left them to work their magic. On the way to her quarters, she gave Winston a treat. The dog settled down in his bed and took a nap while Grace showered and did her hair, brushing it until the golden highlights gleamed. Ponytail or loose? Definitely loose today. She was in that kind of mood.

She slipped into a slim camel-colored skirt and a lightweight cream blouse with delicate capped sleeves. A blue beaded necklace with matching earrings and a bracelet gave the outfit a bit of color.

Now she was ready to face the rest of the day.

Winston rose from his bed and followed her to the reception desk.

A few minutes later, Grace glanced up from filing papers to watch Becca descending the stairs. She was dismayed to see that the young woman still had an air of sadness about her.

Winston seemed to sense Becca's distress, because he padded over to her and whined softly.

Becca set her bag on the floor, then reached down and scratched behind his ears. "You're so sweet, Winston."

"He certainly is," Grace agreed. "Is there something I can do for you?"

"I'm going into town again, and I was wondering if you could recommend some places to check out."

"Of course," Grace said with a smile. "The Heritage Library has a wonderful collection, and the Jackson House Museum is housed in a Victorian mansion. If you're interested in shopping, we have Miss Millie's dress shop, Spool & Thread, and The Book Cottage."

"Those places sound lovely. Thank you." Becca slung her bag over her shoulder and left.

Grace went to the kitchen and set a pitcher of sweet tea and some glasses on a tray. She carried the tray outside and passed the drinks out to the men working diligently on the lawn.

As she turned to go inside, a police car pulled up. Grace left the tray on the front porch and went over to meet Captain Daley.

The captain rolled down his window, but he left the car running.

"What brings you by?" Grace asked. "I hope it's good news."

"Unfortunately, no," Daley answered. "I was on my way to the station and thought I'd swing by and tell you that another historical site on the edge of town was vandalized last night. The Orniston Museum."

He had named one of the oldest houses in the area. It had once been a private residence, but now it was open for tour groups to visit.

"That's awful," Grace said. Vandalism was destructive on so many levels. Not only did it affect the appearance of a place, but it also harmed the spirits of those around it. "Do you have any idea who's responsible?"

"Not yet," the captain admitted. "The investigation is ongoing."

"I can't believe it," she said. "Why would anyone do something like this?"

"That's what we're trying to find out," Daley said. "I suspect it's the work of someone harboring a grudge."

"A grudge against Charlotte and me?" Grace asked, shocked.

"Probably not against you two specifically," the captain said. "I think the fact that only historic sites are being vandalized means it's more likely about a general wish for revenge against Magnolia Harbor. I'll keep you posted."

As Grace watched him drive away, she prayed they'd find the person or people responsible soon. Magnolia Harbor was full of historic sites. If this wasn't stopped, the damage could devastate the community.

9

Becca

"Can I get you anything else?" Angel asked as she set a tall plastic cup filled with unsweetened passion iced tea on the counter.

"No thanks," Becca said. "This should do for now." Her blood sugar level had been slightly elevated this morning, but it hadn't been too much out of the ordinary. Becca was honestly surprised. She'd indulged more yesterday than she had in a long time. Today she was determined to stay on plan and avoid pastries and other sweets, no matter how tantalizing they appeared. "Although I would appreciate a lid for the cup. I can be a klutz."

"You got it." Angel handed her a lid.

Becca returned to the table in the corner that she'd sat at the day before. She opened her laptop and signed into the Wi-Fi.

As she opened the browser, her mind flashed back to meeting Jesse last night on the veranda at the inn. Becca had been surprised and flattered when he had chosen to sit next to her, because most guys were not drawn to her. She was too shy and serious. When Jesse had joined her, she'd felt so awkward that for a moment she'd considered making an excuse and returning to her room. But then he'd started talking. After a few moments, her shyness had fled. She really had enjoyed talking with him.

Until Jesse had mentioned his parents' anniversary party.

Then all her joy had vanished as her ex-fiancé's betrayal smacked her back to reality. The suddenness of the shift had panicked her, and she'd jumped out of her seat and retreated to her room. She knew her actions had stunned Jesse, and she was embarrassed.

Why had she overreacted like that? Would Jesse ever talk to her again? Becca shook her head. It didn't matter anyway. She didn't want any more complications in her life. No, she needed to figure out how to deal with her situation before she could move on with any other plans.

Her phone pinged, jolting her out of her thoughts.

Becca cringed, wondering who had texted her. She really didn't want to know.

She reluctantly reached for her phone and opened the text. It was from Veronica. *Why is Chelsea asking about your fiancé? Are you engaged? I need all the details. Call me.*

Becca started to set her phone back down, intending not to answer yet.

Her phone pinged again. *Don't even think about ignoring me.*

Becca turned off her phone, determined to enjoy one more day before she had to fess up to her lie. She dropped her phone into her laptop bag so she wouldn't keep checking it and feeling guilty.

Forcing her current problem out of her mind, Becca focused on her work. To her surprise, she was able to concentrate better than she had yesterday. The world slipped away as she researched and made notes. A tentative plan of how to organize her research began to form in her mind. Excitement gripped her. She retrieved her notebook and a pen from her bag and started working out a basic outline.

Someone sat down in the chair across from her.

Becca gasped and jumped. "Jesse, you startled me."

"I'm sorry," Jesse said. "I was walking down the street and saw you from the window. Thought I'd say hello." He paused. "Did I say something to offend you last night?"

"No," Becca said, heat blooming in her cheeks. "I mean, I was upset about something, but it had nothing to do with you. I'm sorry for running out like that."

"It's okay," Jesse said. "I was afraid I'd said something wrong. I'm here if you want to talk."

Becca was touched by his concern, especially since they had only met last evening, but she didn't want to unload her problems on him. "I'm all right, but I appreciate the offer."

"I'm guessing you're working on your project," he said, motioning to her laptop and notebook. "Should I leave?"

"I don't mind if you stay," she answered. "I had a good time talking to you last night."

"I did too," Jesse said. "I'm going to order a coffee. Do you want anything?"

"No thanks. I'm set," Becca said, pointing to her tea. "If you have a sweet tooth, they have some excellent pastries here."

"I probably shouldn't indulge." He grinned. "Charlotte's cooking is going to get me in enough trouble."

She laughed.

Jesse left to place his order. He was still limping slightly.

Becca focused on her research while she waited.

He returned with a cup of coffee and a small platter containing a variety of vegetables and hummus. "I thought this should work for a snack if we get hungry."

"Oh, I love hummus."

Jesse sat down and nudged the platter toward Becca. "Help yourself."

"Thanks." She plucked a green pepper wedge off the tray and scooped up some hummus. "This is great."

"It is," he agreed as he took a bite.

"You said you were in the military?" Becca asked.

Jesse nodded. "Army. I served almost two tours, but I was discharged when I got injured. My knee had to be replaced."

"Oh no. I'm so sorry. How were you injured?" She bit her lip. "Or is that rude to ask? I'm sorry."

"I don't mind," he said, waving her apology aside. "My unit was evacuating people from the area after an explosion. When the flames hit something flammable and caused a second explosion, my knee was severely injured by the debris."

"That's awful." Becca clenched her hands together. It must have been terrifying living through such an ordeal. "Did you manage to get everyone out?"

"Yes, we got all twenty-six people out. Three had major burn wounds, and several had cuts and scrapes and suffered from smoke inhalation. But no one died."

"You're a hero," she breathed, her admiration for him skyrocketing. "All of you."

Jesse squirmed in his chair. "No, I was just very lucky. It could have been much worse."

"Stop that," Becca chided him. "Don't dismiss what you did. It was heroic. And lives were saved."

"Okay, I won't argue." He held up his hands as if surrendering. "But seriously, I didn't sign up for the Army for heroic reasons."

Becca leaned her elbows on the table, clasped her hands together, and rested her chin on them. "Tell me why you joined." She couldn't believe she was being so forward, but she wanted to know what had driven Jesse. He wasn't a braggart, and she was impressed by his humble description of the rescue of more than two dozen people. If David saved a life in his work as a doctor, he would make sure that everyone knew he deserved the credit.

The comparison did not put her former fiancé in a good light.

Jesse took a sip of his coffee. He glanced away, but Becca didn't believe he was avoiding her eyes. She had the impression he was getting his thoughts in order. He seemed to be a contemplative man, and she liked that.

He faced Becca. "I have two siblings. Both overachievers. Marlene is the oldest. She was the class valedictorian, and now she's a lawyer and well on her way to becoming a high-powered defense attorney. My brother, Zach, owns a successful accounting business. My parents are very proud of both of them."

Her heart was already breaking for the lost little boy she sensed he'd been.

"I did okay in school," Jesse continued. "It wasn't my thing though, you know? I've always been more of a hands-on kind of guy. So as soon as I graduated from high school, I joined the Army."

She nodded.

"I'm ashamed to say this." Jesse rubbed the back of his neck. "I haven't seen my parents since I enlisted."

"I'm sure they'll be thrilled to see you," Becca said, though she wondered why he hadn't seen his parents in such a long time. But she kept the question to herself, not wanting to pry into the life of someone she'd known for less than twenty-four hours.

He picked up a broccoli floret from the platter. "Anyway, my parents' anniversary party was my brother's idea. I offered to come early to make sure everything was on track, because Zach's business is booming and Marlene is recovering from cancer."

"How sad. I'm glad she's in remission."

"Yeah, me too," he said. "When I found out Marlene had cancer, it put everything else into perspective. None of the other stuff seemed to matter when I realized my sister might not make it. That was when I decided to reconnect with my family."

Becca blinked back tears. Her own sisters drove her nuts, but she never stopped loving them. Even when she was ignoring them. The thought made her hyperaware of the phone in her bag. "I think it's great that your whole family will be getting back together."

"It'll be interesting," Jesse said. "The party marks quite a milestone. My parents have been married for thirty-five years."

Suddenly, her own problems overwhelmed her, and she began to cry. Becca grabbed a napkin and tried to stem the tide of tears, but nothing would hold them back. "Excuse me." She sprang out of her chair and rushed outside, but there was nowhere to escape. Besides, her computer and phone were still inside the coffee shop.

"Hey," Jesse said, coming up behind her. "Angel moved your stuff behind the counter. Let's walk for a bit."

Becca didn't resist when he led her away.

"I don't mean to be nosy, but this is the second time you've bolted when I mentioned my parents' anniversary," he said. "I understand if you don't want to talk, but I'm here if you do."

She stopped and rubbed the tears off her cheeks. "This is so embarrassing."

Jesse handed her a napkin.

"Thanks." Becca accepted it and wiped her face. "Did you grab this off the table?"

"I thought it might come in handy." He shoved his hands into his pockets as they resumed walking. "What do you think? You listened to me. Now it's my turn."

She snorted. "Except your story doesn't end with you doing something really dumb."

He raised an eyebrow and waited.

"I was engaged," Becca finally admitted. "David and I were engaged for over a year, which seems like a long time. Or it did to me. Anyway, a few months ago, I get a text from him. He didn't think we were a good match."

Jesse halted, his jaw dropping. "Are you kidding me? He sent you a text to break off your engagement?"

It was probably petty of her, but the outrage in his voice made her feel a little better. "Not very classy, was it? I was so hurt and embarrassed. We had already ordered the invitations. Thank goodness they hadn't been mailed yet."

"That's awful."

"It was even worse telling my family," Becca said. "My two older sisters—who are both gorgeous, by the way—are married, and they were pressuring me to tie the knot too. My mom has been very vocal in her disappointment. She's all about appearances. It didn't make her happy to tell everyone that her daughter would not be marrying the young doctor she'd been bragging about."

"Your mom should have been relieved that you didn't marry the jerk," Jesse said. "What did your dad say?"

Becca took a deep breath. It was still hard to talk about her father. She missed him so much. "He passed away three years ago. Heart disease."

"I'm sorry."

"My dad wouldn't have liked David." She laughed softly. "He would have seen right through him."

"No wonder you're so broken up," he said gently. "That's a lot of hurt for only a few years."

"There's more," Becca said. "My cousin Chelsea sent me an invitation to her wedding with David."

"Your cousin is marrying your ex-fiancé?" Jesse asked, sounding shocked. "That's harsh."

"To put it mildly."

"Did you know they were dating?" he asked.

"I had no idea," she said. "Chelsea and I have always been close, but we're also competitive. Apparently, I didn't know exactly how competitive she truly is."

"I know it's painful to go through something like this, but—"

"It doesn't excuse what I did," Becca said, cutting him off. "I was so angry and hurt that I accepted the invitation." She paused. "For myself and my fiancé."

"Your fiancé?" Jesse repeated. "You got engaged again?"

Becca stopped in the middle of the sidewalk and dropped her head into her hands. "No, and that's the problem. I lied. I said I was bringing my fiancé to the wedding and sealed the envelope. I realized I was being childish, but I had no intention of ever actually mailing it."

"Then what's the issue? Just don't send it."

"I dropped the envelope at the inn, and Grace found it," she explained. "It was already addressed and stamped, so she mailed it."

The silence lengthened between them.

Finally, he broke it. "Let me get this straight. Your cousin is going to believe that you're engaged and bringing some guy to her wedding."

"One of my sisters texted me earlier to ask about my new fiancé, so Chelsea already knows. It's a mess. It wouldn't be nearly as bad if I only had to confess it to my sisters. But the fact that David and Chelsea will find out I lied is beyond humiliating."

Jesse started walking again, his expression contemplative. "What if you did bring someone to the wedding? You could go, have a good time, and then later tell everyone that it didn't work out. It might be a little less embarrassing to tell them you were unengaged again."

"Unengaged?" she echoed. "Is that even a word?"

"I made it up," he said. "Anyway, that would work, wouldn't it?"

"I suppose, but there's no one I could ask to pretend to be engaged to me for an evening."

Jesse gave her an intense look. "Why not me?"

10

Grace

Later that afternoon, as Grace was making a list of chores she needed to do, the phone on the reception desk rang. She picked up.

"Sorry for bothering you again today," Captain Daley said.

"It's not a bother," Grace said. "What can I do for you?"

"I was planning on stopping by the inn in a little while," the captain answered. "There's someone I'd like to introduce you to. Will you be available?"

"Yes, I'll be here," Grace said, but she wondered why he wouldn't tell her what was going on. She didn't believe he wanted to introduce her to the person responsible for the damage. On the other hand, it wasn't like the captain to be secretive.

"Good. Oh, and if there's a room available at the inn, would you please reserve it?"

Her mouth dropped open. What an odd request for the captain to make. "A couple of our guests had to check out suddenly this morning, so we do have a room available. I'm happy to reserve it, but I'd like to know what's going on."

"Thanks," he said. "I'll explain when I get there."

"I'll see you later." Grace shook her head as she disconnected. There was no use speculating on the captain's unusual request. She had a lot to accomplish today.

The bell above the front door jingled as Winnie walked in.

Winston yipped and ran to her so she could pet him.

"It's wonderful to see you," Grace said. She got up and gave her aunt a hug. "What brings you over?"

"I was wondering if you needed a hand," Winnie said.

"That would be great. Thank you." Not for the first time, Grace marveled at how her aunt always knew when she could use some assistance. Grace had never seen anyone with the ability to sense what someone might need as Winnie did. It was more than a gift.

Many times, Grace had seen Winnie give something to a guest with a vague comment that she thought the item might help them. And invariably it did, although the guest didn't always understand how it would be useful until later. Neither did Grace, but she'd seen her aunt's intuition at work too often to question it.

"Oliver and his crew are making good progress on the lawn," Winnie commented.

"They certainly are," Grace agreed.

Earlier Grace had gone outside to watch them work for a few minutes. Her apprehension about the anniversary party had faded as she saw the ugly ruts disappear. The image of a lush, beautiful lawn serving as the background for such a special occasion blossomed in her mind.

"Everything will be lovely in time for the party," Winnie said.

"I think so too," Grace said. She regarded her aunt's soft lavender dress that went perfectly with her upswept blonde hair. "You look nice."

Winnie laughed, patting her hair. "I'm surprised. I spent the morning with Paisley and her kids. They gave me quite the workout."

Grace chuckled. Winnie and Gus had four grown daughters with families of their own. Amelia, Harper, and Maria all lived out of state, but Paisley still lived in Magnolia Harbor, teaching fifth grade at the local elementary school. She and her husband, Bryson, had two young children, Sam and Monica, who were Winnie's heart.

"How's Gus doing?" Grace asked.

Winnie grinned. "When I left, he was on the phone with someone he'd worked with at the railroad. He hadn't heard from the man in years. It was like listening to a little boy, the way those two carried on." Her voice was rich with fondness for the man she'd been married to for almost half a century.

Grace's heart was heavy in her chest. She'd always wanted that kind of love, but after the fiasco with her former husband, she'd been so emotionally drained that she couldn't even bear to think about romance.

"Are you all right?" Winnie asked, studying Grace's face.

"I'm fine," Grace assured her. "I was just thinking how wonderful it is that you and Gus have been together for so long."

"We love each other," Winnie said. "Even when times have been hard or we've been angry, we always remember that we're in it until death do us part."

Grace bit her lip. "If I'm honest, I suppose I envy you. I always wanted that kind of relationship, and now I'm afraid it's too late."

Winnie gently patted Grace's cheek. "One never knows when love will arrive, dear. Don't shut the door because you think you're too old. Love can come to anyone, no matter the age."

Grace talked about the anniversary party preparations, steering the conversation to a more neutral topic. She mentioned that the flowers had been ordered, and they had already marked off an area on the lawn for the tent and the tables.

"It sounds like everything is coming together," Winnie said, then glanced around. "What can I do?"

"Well, I was jotting down a list of chores," Grace said. "The first thing on the list is refreshing the guest rooms."

"I'll get started," Winnie offered.

"Thanks," Grace said.

Winnie retrieved a basket of cleaning supplies from the closet and went upstairs.

Grace finished her list and was about to follow when the front door opened, the bell above the door jingling. She turned to see Daley and a tall man with short brown hair enter.

Winston raced to greet the men, and Grace joined them.

"Is this a good time to talk?" the captain asked.

"Of course. We can speak privately in the living room." Grace led the two men into the room. Winston followed.

When the men had taken their seats, Grace asked, "Would you like something to eat or drink?"

"No thank you," Daley said.

Grace sat down across from the men, and Winston settled at her feet.

"This is Sergeant Mason Groves," the captain told Grace. "He's here from Rochester, New York."

Grace raised her eyebrows. She doubted that the sergeant had come all the way from New York for their local vandalism issue. "Welcome to Magnolia Harbor. I'm assuming there's a very particular reason I'm being introduced to you."

Groves nodded. "My department has been discreetly looking into the activities of a businessman by the name of William Canfield. Have you ever heard of him?"

"No, the name doesn't ring a bell," Grace replied.

"Have you heard one of your guests talk about William Canfield?" Groves persisted.

She shook her head.

"I didn't really expect that you would have." Groves pulled a phone from his pocket and tapped on the screen, then showed it to Grace. "Have you seen this man?"

Grace examined the image of a handsome man with dark hair and a powerful physique. Again, she shook her head.

Groves scrolled through his phone and showed it to Grace. "What about this woman? I believe she might have been spotted here."

She gasped. "That's Leslie Thomas, one of our guests. Please tell me she's not a criminal."

"I don't believe so," Groves responded. "What we do know is that Ms. Thomas was dating Mr. Canfield. She left town. His phone records show that he tried to call her, but the length of the calls suggest she didn't answer. He left town soon after she did, and we think he may be aware that he was under scrutiny. His phone has since been disconnected. It is my suspicion that he is attempting to find her."

"You think he might show up here?" Grace asked, stunned. "Are Leslie and our other guests in danger?"

"No, I don't think so," Groves said. "He's got a temper, but he's not a violent man as far as we know. His crimes are more along the lines of accepting and offering bribes and some political corruption in regard to local campaigns. When Ms. Thomas went missing, some of his endeavors started to decline. So, he has a good reason for convincing her to come back with him."

"What if she doesn't want to go?" Grace asked. "What if she refuses?"

The sergeant tightened his jaw. "I don't think it would be outside the realm of possibility for Mr. Canfield to forcibly try to take her back to New York in the hopes that she would help improve his numbers in the polls."

"Are you serious?" Grace asked, appalled.

"Unfortunately, yes," Groves said. "His business depends on him, and he has millions of dollars on the line."

A shiver worked its way up her spine. Some people would do unspeakable things for that amount of money.

"I will do my best to ensure the safety of Ms. Thomas and your guests," Groves assured her.

"I'm going to hold you to that," Grace said, then turned to Daley. "In light of our earlier conversation, I'm assuming that Sergeant Groves will be staying here to keep an eye on the situation."

"He will," Daley replied. "When he's not here, I'll have one of my officers on the grounds." He leaned forward. "On another topic, I can't tell you too much, but we have several suspects in the vandalism case."

"That's good news," Grace said. "Will you be making an arrest soon?"

"That's the plan," the captain said. "I'll let you know more details when I can."

"I appreciate the update," Grace said.

"Thanks for your time," Daley said as he stood. "I need to go, but Sergeant Groves will remain here."

"Please let me know if there's anything else I can do," Grace said. She ushered the men out of the room.

Winnie was descending the stairs when they entered the foyer. She warmly greeted Daley. Her blue eyes gleamed with curiosity when she glanced at Sergeant Groves, but she didn't ask any questions. Instead, she gave Grace a look that meant she expected an explanation later, then went to the kitchen.

"Am I allowed to tell Winnie about the situation?" Grace asked.

"Yes, you can tell her and Charlotte too," the captain said. "After all, they need to be aware in order to protect the guests here. But don't mention it to anyone else."

She hesitated, then asked the sergeant, "Will Leslie know why you're here?"

"It's best if she didn't," he responded. "In fact, please treat me as a regular guest and call me Mason or Mr. Groves. I don't want to raise any suspicion, especially if Leslie is in touch with Canfield."

"Of course," Grace said. "Please join the other guests on the back veranda at six for hospitality hour. Would you like me to show you to your room?"

Daley left, and Grace showed the sergeant to the recently vacated Dogwood Suite, then headed to the kitchen.

She found Winnie helping Charlotte ready the appetizers and desserts for hospitality hour.

"Who was that man with Daley?" Winnie asked as she arranged the cupcakes on a colorful plate.

Charlotte and Winnie paused in their work as Grace explained who Mason was and what was going on with Leslie and her ex-boyfriend.

"Oh no," Charlotte said. "I feel terrible for Leslie."

"I do too," Grace said. "It's such a shock."

The three women continued to discuss the situation as they finished preparing the food. Then they carried the bottles of wine, platters, and trays to the back veranda.

"Are you staying for hospitality hour?" Charlotte asked Winnie.

"I'd love to," she answered. "I think I'll call Gus and ask him to join us."

"Sounds great," Charlotte said.

As Grace returned to the kitchen for a pitcher of sweet tea, she heard the bell above the front door jingle. She detoured to the foyer and saw Spencer walk inside.

A glow of pleasure warmed her, and she smiled. "What a pleasant surprise. Will you stay for hospitality hour?"

"No thanks." Spencer shifted and cleared his throat. "I'm here to pick up Olivia. We're going out to dinner to catch up."

Heat flooded her face, and she couldn't think of anything else to say.

"Spencer, *mon cher*!" Olivia descended the stairs and hurried over to Spencer. She kissed him on both cheeks, a decidedly French gesture. "I'm ready whenever you are."

Grace pasted a smile on her face, but the disappointment stabbing her made it hard to keep it in place. "Have a nice evening."

"I'm sure we will," Olivia said, resting a hand on Spencer's arm. "I can't wait to check out The Tidewater. It sounds so romantic."

Spencer gave Grace a weak smile, then escorted Olivia out the door.

When Grace turned, she saw Becca walking toward her. "Good evening. Will you be joining us for hospitality hour?"

"I wouldn't miss it," Becca answered. She glanced around. "Have you seen Jesse?"

Before she could reply, Jesse ran down the stairs. "Sorry I'm late. I was talking to my brother and lost track of time."

"No problem," Becca said.

"Are you ready?" Jesse asked, holding out his arm.

Grace blinked. It appeared that the Magnolia Harbor Inn was once again working its magic in the lives of their guests.

"We'll see you on the veranda," Becca told Grace.

When they were gone, Grace retrieved the pitcher of sweet tea from the kitchen. As she carried it to the veranda, she thought about Spencer. She didn't like to admit that it hurt to see him taking Olivia out to dinner. Grace shook her head. Spencer had been ready to deepen their relationship, and she had put a stop to it.

She couldn't blame him for wanting to move on.

Without her.

11

Leslie

When Leslie walked onto the veranda Wednesday evening for hospitality hour, she noticed Becca and Jesse sitting close together. Leslie wanted to say hello, but she hated to interrupt their private conversation. She hesitated in the doorway, wondering what to do.

Then Becca glanced up and grinned at Leslie, beckoning her to join them.

Leslie smiled back, feeling her shoulders relax, and approached their table. "I hope you had a good day."

Becca nodded. "I got some work done, and Jesse and I hung out at a coffee shop for a while. How about you?"

"It was productive," Leslie said vaguely. She wasn't ready to admit that she'd assisted Charlotte with the appetizers and desserts. What if everything was awful? But she knew it wasn't. They had sampled all of it, and she had been especially pleased with how well the cannoli turned out. Leslie felt she had done well, but the idea of watching virtual strangers eating the food she'd made was unsettling.

That was when Leslie realized that she had never let herself be vulnerable like this before. Nothing she'd ever done had been put before strangers to judge. She'd always had her family's name or Will's wealth and reputation to protect her against any harsh words or critical assessments. Even when people had said something negative about her, she felt safe because they weren't seeing her. Not really.

Here at the inn, all anyone saw was Leslie Thomas. No one knew her family or that her ex-boyfriend was a force to be reckoned with.

Grace invited everyone to help themselves to the food and drinks.

Charlotte stood at the buffet table. "We have vegetables with avocado dip, prosciutto rolls, bacon-wrapped dates with almonds, ricotta crostini with chestnut honey, cannoli, and chocolate cupcakes with caramel ganache and coconut. We also have wine, coffee, and sweet tea."

"Are you getting anything?" Becca asked Leslie.

She shook her head. "I'm not hungry. Please go ahead."

Becca and Jesse went to the buffet table and made their selections. A moment later, Winnie and Gus followed suit.

As Leslie watched them sit down with their plates, she felt sick, wondering what they would think when they tried the food. She seriously considered retreating to her room, then chided herself. She wasn't a coward, and she wouldn't run away. It was too important. If she had any hope of starting a new career, she needed to see this through.

Movement at the door caught her attention, and she turned to see a man entering the veranda. He was tall and physically fit with well-toned arms, and he had short brown hair. Leslie had never seen him before, and she wondered who he was. Maybe he was a new guest or a friend of the innkeepers.

The man's expression was serious as he scanned the room.

Leslie stifled a gasp. She was familiar with the look. The man appeared to be a police officer. Will had frequently taken her to functions where he had hobnobbed with cops and lawyers, so she had become accustomed to the stance and actions of policemen. While she never detected anything more than politeness between the police and Will, she worried that he might have had some influence with local law enforcement. That might explain why Will had gotten away with his criminal lifestyle for so long.

The problem was she'd only seen Will talking to cops in social settings, so she had no proof of any illegal activities. But she was afraid to go to the police and risk the chance that they wouldn't believe her. Even worse, they could report it back to Will.

Her thoughts shrieked to a halt when the man turned and stared straight into her eyes. He held her gaze for a couple of seconds before looking away.

Leslie let out her breath. For one frightening moment, she'd felt as if the man had recognized her. But she'd never seen him before, so surely that was ridiculous.

Then the man went over to the buffet table to fill a plate.

"I trust everyone is enjoying the appetizers," Charlotte said.

Leslie braced herself for their reactions.

"They're amazing," Jesse responded, holding up a prosciutto roll.

"I love the ricotta crostini," Winnie said.

Leslie smiled. Little did they know that she had assisted the chef.

Charlotte winked at Leslie.

Her smile vanished. Panicked, Leslie shook her head in a silent plea. She didn't want any recognition.

"Thank you for the kind words," Charlotte continued. "But I did not make the delicacies alone. I am very pleased to announce that we have a new cook in our midst. She's a beginner, but I'm sure that we will see her achieve great things in the culinary arts in the future." She grinned. "Leslie, would you please stand for a round of applause?"

If Leslie could have slithered to the floor and crawled out unnoticed, she would have. But she was trapped. Her mother had trained her to be gracious, so Leslie pasted on a bright smile and stood.

The others clapped and congratulated her.

Becca smiled at Leslie, but she appeared concerned. She clearly understood that Leslie did not want the attention.

The spot between her shoulder blades prickled. Leslie glanced over her shoulder, and her gaze clashed with the cop's.

The man scrutinized her briefly. Then he lifted his glass of sweet tea toward her as if toasting. Was he mocking her?

Lifting her chin, Leslie deliberately ignored him. She was completely unnerved.

Or so she told herself.

Charlotte walked over to Leslie. "The appetizers are a huge hit. Great work. You can be my sous-chef any day."

"Thanks again for the cooking lesson," Leslie said. "I learned so much."

Over Charlotte's shoulder, Leslie saw Grace introducing the man to the other guests. Leslie didn't want to meet him, so she said good night to those around her and retreated to her room.

That night, sleep eluded her. Her mind was torn between the marvel that her first attempt at cooking had been a success and the distress that roiled up when she remembered the cop's gaze locked on hers.

It wasn't attraction. At least she didn't think it was. The man acted as if he knew who she was. Could he be in league with Will? Was that possible? Will hadn't known where she was going. How could he? She hadn't even known until she arrived.

She'd have to be careful the next couple of days. She was reluctant to run again now that she'd finally found a purpose and a haven. And chances were that she was being paranoid.

No, Leslie would stay at the inn. At least for now.

But she'd have to be ready to leave at a moment's notice.

When Leslie woke up the next morning, the sun was streaming in through her window. She was hungry, but she was reluctant to join the others for breakfast in the dining room. She didn't want to see that cop again.

But she had to eat. First, though, she decided to make her preparations. Just in case.

Leslie swiftly repacked her clothes, then frowned. If she needed to run, she might not have time to retrieve her suitcase from the room. Well, if that happened, she'd have to buy new clothes. It wouldn't be an issue. She had money, and the clothes she'd brought with her had no sentimental value. She'd done that on purpose, in case she had to leave them somewhere.

Suddenly, she remembered her car. Would anyone recognize it? Or had someone already seen it? Leslie grimaced. There was nothing she could do about it now. At least her car was parked at the inn, so the odds of anyone noticing it were slim.

She couldn't worry about it. It was too late to fix it anyway. Even if she had gotten a rental car, that might have raised more red flags, especially if Will's friends in law enforcement were tracking her credit cards.

Satisfied that she'd thought of everything, she went to the dining room.

Grace and Charlotte were putting the finishing touches on the buffet table, and Becca, Jesse, and Olivia were grabbing plates. The cop wasn't around. For the first time that morning, she felt like she could take a full breath.

Leslie selected stuffed French toast and fresh fruit, then joined Becca and Jesse at the table.

"Would anyone like coffee or orange juice?" Charlotte asked.

"Coffee, please," Leslie said.

Charlotte filled her cup, and Leslie thanked her. The food was delicious as usual, but Leslie found herself watching the door to the inn, which made it hard to focus on the pleasant conversation and the wonderful food.

Eventually, she couldn't stand her own jumpiness anymore. She thanked her hostesses for breakfast and hurried to her suite, only to stand in the center of the room and stare around her. What should she do now?

Even though her room was more than comfortable, she would go crazy sitting at the inn all day with this much nervous energy coursing through her. Maybe she could go to the library and search for information about Will. She would rather use a public computer because she feared her phone might give her location away. If she browsed for her town news and not Will specifically, it wouldn't trigger any red flags, right?

Plan firmly in mind, Leslie grabbed her purse and went downstairs.

Grace greeted her from the reception desk. "Can I help you?"

"Is there a public library in town?" Leslie asked.

"The Heritage Library is on Willow Street." Grace took a map from behind the counter and gave it to Leslie. "It's one block over from Main Street in the historic district."

"Thanks," Leslie said. She examined the map and noticed there was a shuttle that went to downtown Magnolia Harbor.

Leslie hurried outside and waited for the shuttle. When it arrived, she boarded and sat down. The ride was short, and soon she was strolling through the downtown area to the Heritage Library. At first, her steps were brisk. As she took note of the cobblestone streets and the historic buildings, she slowed down to admire her surroundings. Leslie delighted in the enchanting sights and spent a few minutes snapping pictures. She might never visit this lovely town again, and she didn't intend to forget anything.

When Leslie neared the library, she took out her camera once more. The two-story brick building featured tall arched windows, marble steps, and a majestic entrance. It was an exquisite example of architecture. A metal sign declared that the library had been built through the generosity of Andrew Carnegie.

Finally, she managed to draw herself away from exploring and went inside to focus on her quest.

An older woman with short gray hair sat behind the semicircular circulation desk. "Welcome to the Heritage Library. I'm Phyllis Gendel. How may I help you?"

"I was wondering if I could use one of your computers for research," Leslie said.

"Of course. Right this way." Phyllis rounded the desk and ushered her to a bank of computers.

"Thank you." Stomach clenching with nerves, Leslie sat down at a computer and began her search. She started with the day she'd left. Nothing there. That was encouraging. The second day was the same.

On the third day, however, she came across an article that made her stomach twist into knots. A local businessman and aspiring politician had vanished. Even before she saw his name, she knew it was Will. She scoffed at the implication that he was a victim of foul play. No, he was searching for her.

But he wouldn't find her.

On the next page, there was an article so brief she almost missed it. As she scanned the story, Will's name jumped out at her. The reporter stated that the police suspected that Will was involved with sabotaging a local election.

Leslie's heart sank. Although she hadn't been aware of it at the time, she now knew that Will was capable of that and more. She had been so blind. He'd been using the respectability and connections of her family name to carry out his own despicable agenda.

Will didn't love Leslie, and he never had. To him, she had simply been a way to deceive and commit crimes without repercussions.

How long had he played her? For the entirety of their relationship? It wouldn't surprise her. Not anymore.

Disgusted, Leslie stood and walked to the front door. She thanked Phyllis again, then left the library. She noticed a man outside, talking to a couple on the sidewalk. Her pulse sped up, and her hands grew clammy.

She didn't need to see his face to know it was the officer she'd seen at hospitality hour last evening. What was he doing here? Was he following her?

Spinning on her heel, Leslie walked in the opposite direction, struggling to keep her breathing under control. Even though she tried to act casual, she glanced over her shoulder. The cop was still talking to the couple. In fact, he didn't so much as look in her direction. Maybe she was overacting, and his presence in town was only a coincidence.

She continued walking for a while, then slowed down. She chided herself for feeling paranoid. The man hadn't spoken to her. For all she knew, he hadn't even seen her. So what if there were police at the inn? It would be perfectly normal for officers to show up at the scene of a crime, such as the vandalism on the lawn. This particular officer might simply be staying there on vacation.

Not sure what else to do, Leslie spent the next couple of hours perusing the quaint stores on Main Street. She lost herself in the shelves at The Book Cottage and browsed the beautiful clothes at Miss Millie's dress shop. Though not a crafter, Leslie stopped at Spool & Thread and wandered around the aisles packed with fabrics, tools, notions, and other supplies.

When Leslie left the fabric shop, she spotted a restaurant called

Why Thai. She'd never eaten Thai food before. Leslie couldn't resist the lure of trying new dishes. She rushed to the restaurant.

The place was busy, but Leslie was able to snag a small table.

Within a couple of minutes, the waitress came over and gave Leslie a menu. "Can I get you something to drink?"

"A cup of tea, please," Leslie said.

"Coming up," the waitress said, then hurried away.

Leslie scanned the menu. It was hard to decide, because everything sounded amazing.

Several times she wondered if she could cook any of the dishes. She grabbed a notepad and a pen from her purse and jotted down several items that she wanted to research later.

The waitress returned with her tea and took her order. Leslie had finally decided on spring rolls and chicken pad thai.

While Leslie waited, she jotted down more notes. Ideas were brewing about what kind of career she wanted to create. There were so many choices.

Soon the waitress delivered her meal. "Let me know if you need anything else."

Leslie had never enjoyed eating alone so much. She savored the spring rolls and chicken pad thai and ate every single bite, taking notes on the textures and flavor combinations. When she paid her bill and left a tip, she was glad she'd stopped here for lunch.

As soon as Leslie returned to the inn, she was greeted by Winston, his tail wagging. She got down on her knees to pet him, and his whole body quivered in delight.

"Winston really likes you," Grace commented, walking into the foyer.

Leslie grinned. "I like him too. I'm thinking about adopting a dog."

"They need a lot of care, but they bring so much joy." Grace paused. "I was getting ready to take him for a walk, but maybe you'd like to do it."

Winston barked, running in a circle around Leslie.

Leslie laughed. "I think he understands. I would love to take him. Where should I go?"

Grace handed Leslie his leash and suggested they walk by the lake. "There's a nice path over there."

"Come on, boy," Leslie said, clipping the leash on Winston's collar. "This is going to be fun."

Winston led the way outside.

While they strolled by the lake, Leslie mused on how much pleasure she got simply from walking the dog and how much his presence comforted her.

"Maybe we could do this again," she told Winston as they walked back. When they entered the inn, she unclipped the leash from his collar and watched as he ran to Grace.

"Thanks for walking him," Grace said.

"It was my pleasure." Satisfied, Leslie headed upstairs. She was halfway to the second floor when she realized she was still holding Winston's leash. Leslie went downstairs to return it to Grace, but she paused when she heard voices. Winnie and Grace were speaking in hushed tones.

"Is her boyfriend really searching for her?" Winnie asked.

"That's why Sergeant Groves is here from Rochester, New York," Grace replied.

Leslie's breath stalled at the words. Were they talking about her? They had to be. After all, who else had a connection to New York and an ex-boyfriend who was attempting to find her?

"I didn't get a chance to talk to Sergeant Groves at hospitality hour last night," Winnie said. "But it's comforting to know that he's staying at the inn."

So Sergeant Groves was the cop who had stared at her at hospitality hour, and he was definitely here because of her. Leslie didn't stay to listen to the rest of the conversation. After dropping the leash on the reception desk, she rushed to her room.

Leslie should leave now. She shook her head, forcing herself to remain calm, even as her paranoia ratcheted up. While she paced her room, trying to calm down enough to think rationally, she heard measured footsteps out in the hallway.

She peeked out the peephole. Nothing. She wasn't sure what she'd been expecting. Maybe for Sergeant Groves to be standing there.

Despite her denials, Leslie couldn't abandon the idea that Groves was watching her. It was possible he was using her as some sort of trap to catch Will. She'd have to sneak out when he wasn't watching. He might follow her or try to prevent her from leaving.

Leslie needed to escape, but it would take stealth. She had to be ready to go as soon as the right moment arrived.

Becca

Becca looked at Jesse as he examined the woodwork of the staircase at the Jackson House Museum. It was incredible to think that they had met only two days ago.

When Jesse caught her staring at him, he winked.

She flushed and turned away, but she was smiling. Simply being in his presence made her spirit sing.

Was it possible to fall in love again?

Becca wasn't sure, but after being around Jesse, she realized that she had never felt quite this way about David. When David had talked about his work, she had felt no connection. It was all about him. He had only needed her to nod at the appropriate places and make noncommittal comments.

David had also dismissed her job. Becca realized how often he had disparaged teaching, particularly elementary school. She now understood that he believed that teaching really didn't take any true skill. How many times had he belittled her for not living up to her full potential? How many times had he told her that after they married, she would no longer need to work in that dead-end job?

On the other hand, Jesse seemed to enjoy hearing her discuss her work. Instead of talking over her or changing the subject, he asked questions and listened.

Her heart was very much in danger.

Becca should back off and focus on her master's project. Besides, wasn't she still healing from her breakup? She no longer trusted her own judgment as far as men were concerned. Jesse also had some family drama that he still needed to work through.

"We should think about lunch," Jesse said. He grabbed her hand as they walked to the next room.

Her entire arm felt warm from the tingles shooting up from their joined fingers. "Where would you like to go?" Becca really didn't care where they went. She was just happy to spend time with him.

"Grace mentioned Aunt Patsy's Porch," Jesse said. "Apparently it's Southern-style home cooking with the best pie in a hundred miles."

"It gets my vote," Becca said.

"Mine too. I can't wait to try the pie." Jesse consulted the map on his phone. "It's a good thing you have your car. It would probably be a miserable walk in this heat." He smiled. "Let's go."

As they climbed into the car, Becca remembered his idea for another place they should go together—the wedding. She was quiet on the drive to the restaurant.

"Is something bothering you?" Jesse asked, sounding concerned.

"I was thinking about this story we've fabricated."

After Jesse had offered to pretend to be Becca's fiancé at Chelsea and David's wedding, they had planned it all out. Next week, Jesse would drive to Becca's house, and she'd introduce him to her family. Then they'd go to the wedding together on Friday.

"What about it?" Jesse asked.

"I feel guilty about lying," Becca answered, "and I hate for you to be a part of this scheme."

"It'll be okay," Jesse said. "It's only one day. Then everything will go back to normal."

Becca nodded, though she still had her doubts. If they didn't go through with this plan, she'd have to attend the wedding alone. Or not go at all, which would garner even more gossip and the same amount of pity.

As she considered the situation, she couldn't help but wonder if they could have a real future together. Immediately she chided herself for her foolish musings. She should enjoy the time she had with Jesse instead of speculating about a vague future.

They parked outside Aunt Patsy's Porch, and Jesse pointed out the special features of the white clapboard building with a wide wraparound veranda. Becca had to admit that it was adorable.

Jesse opened the door for her and waited for her to enter first.

Becca glanced around the restaurant. The walls were lined with vintage photographs and shelves filled with a variety of antiques. The tables and chairs were delightfully mismatched, and there were pretty lace curtains on the windows. She was charmed.

"Please seat yourselves," a waitress said as she hurried past them with a tray.

Jesse pointed to a corner table in front of the window. "How about there?"

"Sure," Becca said. She was surprised that Jesse had asked her opinion about something so minor. David wouldn't have done that. She needed to stop comparing the two men, because it would only drive her crazy. Plus, she was not Jesse's girlfriend in real life. She needed to remember that.

Jesse ushered her over to the table and held a chair out for her.

Becca sat down, impressed with what a gentleman he was. "Thank you."

A different waitress came to their table and gave them menus. "Welcome to Aunt Patsy's. I'm Molly. Can I get you something to drink?"

Jesse gestured to Becca.

"I'll have a glass of unsweetened iced tea, please," she said.

"Of course," Molly answered, then turned to Jesse. "And you?"

"Root beer."

"Coming right up," Molly promised. When she returned with their drinks, she took a notepad and a pencil out of her pocket. "What can I get you?"

"I'll have the baked chicken with a Caesar salad," Becca said.

Molly nodded and jotted it down.

"And I'll have a sirloin steak, medium, with sweet potatoes and a cup of minestrone soup," Jesse said.

"Got it." Molly wrote in her notepad and collected their menus. "It'll be ready shortly."

When they were alone again, there was a moment of awkward silence.

They'd spent the last couple of days together. They had laughed, and he had comforted her when she had cried. They had even held hands. Yet Becca had never felt as though they were on a date. Not until this moment. Suddenly, all thoughts flew right out of her head. She couldn't think of a single smart or funny thing to say.

"Check it out," Jesse said, motioning to one of the vintage photographs on the wall. "Here's a picture of Magnolia Harbor from back in the day."

Relieved for a new topic of conversation, Becca latched on to it. As she examined the picture, she noticed a familiar Victorian mansion. "That must be the Jackson House Museum."

Jesse nodded.

Becca picked up her iced tea and took a sip. She sighed without meaning to.

"Thinking about David?" Jesse asked.

"I'm fine. Mostly, I feel dumb for getting duped." She toyed with her straw. "Anyway, I don't want to talk about David. I gave him too much attention for far too long. So let's change the subject."

His expression brightened. "I'm glad you feel that way. Except for one thing. You are not dumb. You are a smart, gifted woman with drive and a loving heart. He didn't deserve you."

Becca swallowed past the sudden lump in her throat. "Thanks for saying that. It means a lot."

"You're very welcome," Jesse said. He gave her a stern look. "But I am concerned about one thing."

"Oh?" She raised her eyebrows. "What would that be?"

He pointed at her glass. "You're drinking unsweetened tea in South Carolina. Is that even legal?"

Becca giggled, then put her hand over her mouth. She never giggled. "Sorry. I like my tea unsweetened. Besides, I have diabetes."

"I'm so sorry," Jesse said. "How did I not know this? We've been eating together the last couple of days, and I never even clued in."

"It's okay that you didn't watch what I ate," she teased. "That would have been a little creepy."

He chuckled, then looked thoughtful. "Now that you mention it, I noticed that you stuck to the veggie tray last night at hospitality hour and you didn't eat dessert. But I've never seen you take insulin shots or anything."

"I don't need insulin. I'm type 2, but my case is pretty mild. I watch my carbs, avoid eating too much processed food, and check my blood sugar every day before breakfast. I also take medicine, and I try to keep hydrated."

"It's great the way you take charge of it," Jesse said.

Molly breezed over and delivered their orders. They both leaned back to allow the waitress to place their steaming plates in front of them. The aromas wafting from the dishes made Becca's stomach grumble.

"Enjoy," Molly said and walked away.

"Wow, this is a lot of food." Becca spread her napkin on her lap before picking up her fork. "I never eat like this for lunch."

"It's a special occasion." Jesse cut into his steak and took a bite. "Delicious."

Becca tried her chicken. "Mine's delicious too."

They dug into the food, but this time, the silence was companionable rather than awkward.

"Tell me about growing up in Pennsylvania," Jesse said after a few minutes.

Becca shrugged. "What is there to say? We lived in town, but I grew up near farm country. It was normal to see cows, horses, and other animals on the way to school. Many of my friends raised livestock for their 4-H projects. What about Ohio?"

He smiled. "I grew up close to Columbus, so I didn't see as much farm country." He took a sip of his root beer. "I've driven through Pennsylvania before. There were a lot of hills. Ohio is pretty flat."

The minutes flew by as they discussed their childhoods and enjoyed the food.

Molly came over to take their empty plates. "Would you like dessert? We have the best pie in a hundred miles."

Becca and Jesse exchanged grins.

"A slice of apple pie, please," Jesse said.

"Good choice," Molly said, then turned to Becca. "What can I get you?"

"Do you have any sugar-free desserts?"

"We have raspberry sorbet, frozen yogurt, and pumpkin pie," Molly replied.

"I can't pass up the best pie in the area," Becca said. "I'll have a slice of pumpkin."

While enjoying their slices of pie, they talked about their favorite music and movies. Becca was pleased to discover that they had similar tastes in the arts.

When they were done, Jesse picked up the check.

"You don't have to pay for all of it," Becca objected. "I have money with me."

Jesse covered her hand with his. "I'd really like this to be my treat to you."

She nodded, too full of emotion for words.

He might not have said as much, but she read it in his eyes. This hadn't been simply a meal between two new friends. This was a date between two people who were interested in getting to know each other.

Becca was in so much trouble.

Grace

Grace smiled as she surveyed the spacious lawn with Winston at her side.

Oliver and his crew had finished their repairs. The tracks had been smoothed out, and the yard was pristine. When the guests arrived, they wouldn't see a single blade of grass out of place.

"It's perfect," Grace told Oliver. "I can't thank you enough for all your hard work."

"It was my pleasure," he said. "Let me know if you need anything else."

"I will," Grace promised. "Thanks again."

Oliver patted Winston on the head, then jogged over to his truck and drove away.

Satisfied, Grace returned to the inn and made her way to the kitchen with Winston tagging along.

Charlotte was stirring a pot on the stove, and Leslie was chopping vegetables at the counter.

Her sister glanced up. "Is the yard back to normal?"

"Actually, I think it looks even better than before," Grace said. "Oliver and his team are amazing."

"They certainly are," Charlotte agreed.

Grace scanned the kitchen. "Can I help?"

"We have everything under control for hospitality hour," Charlotte said, then smiled at Leslie. "I have a terrific helper."

"And I have a terrific teacher," Leslie said.

"Oh, Dean and I are going out for a late dinner tonight at Turner's Lakeside Grill," Charlotte told her sister. "Don't worry. We're not leaving until after hospitality hour."

"I can handle it if you want to leave early," Grace said.

Charlotte shook her head. "Dean has to stay at the restaurant anyway."

"Have a great time," Grace said. "If you don't need anything, I'll be tidying up the living room."

Grace left the kitchen. As she crossed the foyer, Olivia walked through the front door.

"Good afternoon," Grace said.

"What a glorious day," Olivia replied, beaming. "I had a productive meeting, and now I'm ready to unwind."

"Are you joining us for hospitality hour this evening?" Grace asked.

"I'd love to, but I already have plans," Olivia said, her eyes sparkling.

"Have a good time," Grace said.

"I'm sure I will." Olivia grinned, then walked away.

Grace tried to ignore the sinking feeling in the pit of her stomach. She knew that Olivia's plans involved Spencer.

14

Grace

After breakfast Friday morning, Grace joined Charlotte and Winnie in the kitchen.

Winston made the rounds, going to each of the women and basking in their attention.

Without a word, Charlotte poured a cup of coffee and pushed it toward Grace.

"Thanks." Grace picked up the cup and lifted it, breathing in the rich aroma before taking a careful sip. It was still a tad too hot, but it was delicious. She blew on it before taking another sip. "Have you heard from Edible Delights?"

They often hired the local catering company when hosting events that were too large for the three of them to handle, such as the anniversary party.

Charlotte nodded. "They'll be over tomorrow morning to start setting up the buffet tables and prepping the food."

"How many people are we expecting at this party?" Winnie asked.

"Around fifty," Grace replied.

"My goodness, that's a big crowd," Winnie said. "I know Jesse has a room here, but where's everyone else staying?"

"Dean mentioned that some of the guests reserved rooms at The Tidewater," Charlotte said.

"I believe that many of the attendees are local," Grace said. "So they won't need a hotel."

The ladies went over the list of chores that needed to be

completed before the party and split the duties between them. Grace planned to meet the setup crew due to arrive soon and refresh the guest rooms, Charlotte needed to work on the appetizers for this evening's hospitality hour, and Winnie headed out the door to man the reception desk.

"I'll be outside waiting for the crew to arrive," Grace said as she grabbed her coffee.

"Can I talk to you for a moment first?" Charlotte asked.

"Of course," Grace said, studying her sister's anxious expression. "What's on your mind?"

Charlotte hesitated. "It's about dinner last night. Dean and I weren't the only ones at Turner's. Spencer was there too."

"He had Olivia with him, didn't he?" Grace asked, even though she already knew the answer.

"Yes, and they looked pretty cozy," Charlotte said softly.

Grace laughed, but it sounded false to her own ears. "Spencer and Olivia have been friends since college. They went to dinner at The Tidewater the other night to catch up."

"I know what I saw," Charlotte insisted. "Are they old flames?"

Grace made a face. She really detested that expression. "Yes, Spencer and Olivia dated in college, but they're just friends now." She hoped that was all they were.

"I hate to tell you this, but Olivia was not giving off 'just friends' vibes," Charlotte said. "She was obviously flirting with him."

"I'm not sure what to say," Grace admitted. "I'm the one who put the brakes on our relationship, so it's really none of my business who Spencer has dinner with."

"I'm sorry about all this." Charlotte gave Grace a hug. "Maybe I shouldn't have said anything, but I thought you should know."

"It's all right," Grace said. "Thanks for telling me."

"I'm always here if you want to talk," Charlotte said as she removed ingredients from the fridge.

Grace left her sister to cook, then headed outside with Winston. It was a blessing that they had so much to do for the party. She needed something to keep her mind occupied today. She hadn't told Charlotte, but earlier that morning, Olivia had told Grace that she planned to surprise Spencer at his house after her business meeting. She had asked Grace for ideas on good picnic spots.

Grace had managed to be gracious, but Olivia was getting on her last nerve. And that wasn't fair. Olivia had no idea that she was hurting Grace.

Winston found a patch of sun and stretched out on the grass.

Two trucks arrived, and several men exited.

Grace greeted the men from the rental company and showed them where to set up the tables and chairs and the large tent covered in tulle instead of canvas.

As Grace supervised their work, she noticed a flash out of the corner of her eye. She turned to the bushes but didn't see anything out of the ordinary. That was odd. Moving closer, she glanced down and spotted something small and gold peeking out from under the bushes.

Bending down, she carefully picked up the object that was no bigger than a quarter and brushed off the dirt.

It was a varsity pin, the kind that high school students were awarded when they lettered in a sport. The pin resembled the one her son had worn on his varsity jacket years ago. But this pin appeared much newer. Plus, it had the new logo Harbor High School had adopted within the last few years.

Grace thought back. There hadn't been any Harbor High School students staying at the inn recently, and she couldn't think of any reason for students to be on the property. Had the vandal dropped it? She reached for her cell phone and dialed the Magnolia Harbor Police Department.

Dolly Batten, the dispatcher, answered.

"Good morning. It's Grace Porter. Is Captain Daley available?"

"Yes, I'll patch you through," Dolly said.

A moment later, the captain asked, "What can I do for you?"

"I found what looks like a varsity pin near the area that was vandalized," Grace answered. "Do you think it belongs to the person who damaged our property?"

"That's a possibility," he said. "Can you tell what sport it's from?"

Grace examined the pin. "Baseball."

"I'll send someone out to collect it," Daley said. "This may be the break we need."

"I hope so." After disconnecting, Grace slipped the tiny pin into her pocket. She didn't dare put it anywhere else out of fear that it would get lost. It was a miracle she had seen it in the first place. As she watched the crew work, she kept patting her pocket, making sure she could still feel the small pin tucked inside.

Twenty nerve-racking minutes later, a police car made its way up the long drive.

"Finally." Grace was sure she'd sprouted at least three gray hairs while waiting.

The car parked, and Officer Brittany Holmes emerged. She left the car running as she jogged over to Grace.

"I'm here to pick up some evidence from you." With her curly auburn hair pulled back in a bushy ponytail, Officer Holmes appeared far too young to be sporting the sharp police uniform. Her hazel eyes were clear, and there was a light dusting of freckles across her nose. Despite her youthful appearance, she was a fine officer, and she was able to keep her cool in dicey situations.

"I found this in the bushes." Grace dug the pin out of her pocket and handed it to the officer.

"Thanks. I'll get it to the captain ASAP," the officer promised. "We're all anxious to stop the vandalism." She hurried to her car and drove away.

Grace and Winston headed inside. Winnie was still at the reception desk.

"How are things going?" her aunt asked.

"The rental company is setting up the tables and the tent," Grace answered, then told her about the varsity pin she'd discovered.

"I hope this helps the police find the vandal," Winnie said.

"Me too," Grace agreed as she retrieved the cleaning supplies. "I'm going to tackle the guest rooms."

As Grace worked, she had a hard time getting the pin out of her mind. Part of her was sad that a teenager appeared to be responsible for the vandalism. This kind of crime would definitely be a mark against the person as he or she applied for schools and jobs. But she would be relieved to see an end to the destruction around town, no matter who the perpetrator was. Defacing property was not something to be taken lightly.

Grace returned to the main floor of the inn as her cell phone rang. It was Captain Daley.

"We took the pin to the high school," Daley said. "The baseball coach confirmed that it was a pin issued in the last two years to a first-year letterman. Which told us that it belonged to someone who was still a student."

"Did you discover who it belonged to?" Grace asked.

"Yes, but I can't give you any specific details yet," he answered. "The suspect is a minor, and his parents are furious."

"I completely understand. I'm just glad to know it's over."

"The thing is, we don't believe he was acting alone," the captain continued. "In fact, I don't think he was the one who did any of the damage. He was probably more of a lookout. Unfortunately, he's not talking. Kids don't like to rat out their buddies."

"What will you do now?" Grace asked.

"His parents are coming in," he said. "They might prove to be more helpful."

"I really appreciate all your hard work on this."

"Of course."

Charlotte walked into the room and headed her way.

Grace covered the mouthpiece of the phone with her hand. "It's the captain. They found one of the vandals."

Charlotte smiled. "You tell him that when this is over, I'll make a peach cobbler for him and his officers."

Grace relayed Charlotte's message.

Daley chuckled. "Please tell your sister that I'll hold her to it."

"Will do." Grace disconnected and turned to Charlotte. "Did you need me?"

"Winnie talked to the florist before she went home. The flowers will be here in the morning."

Grace sighed in relief. "This is all going to work out."

Charlotte nodded. "Even the weather forecast is cooperating. Clear skies the next three days. No sign of rain. It'll be warm but dry."

"I'll take it," Grace said. "If it does rain, we still have the barn."

"True, but I know the family really wants an outdoor party," Charlotte said. She bit her lip.

"What's on your mind?" Grace asked, hoping it wasn't something else about Spencer and Olivia.

"I'm sorry that I upset you when I mentioned Spencer," Charlotte said. "It was never my intention. I want you to be happy. You deserve it."

"To be fair, you only confirmed something I already knew," Grace said, giving her sister a hug. "I'm glad that you have my back, though."

Her heart overflowed with gratitude. No matter what happened with her and Spencer, she was so thankful to have family and friends who loved her and would always support her.

Winston plopped down at her feet and whined softly.

Grace smiled as she scooped him up and held him close. She couldn't forget about her faithful dog who always cheered her up.

She remembered Olivia's expression when she was talking about Spencer and felt the corners of her mouth turn down. Not even Winston could make that okay.

15

Becca

Becca and Jesse sat on a bench at the inn, taking in the beauty and tranquility of Lake Haven. Charlotte had provided them with a basket of goodies, including oatmeal raisin cookies, fresh fruit, and bottles of water.

Becca leaned back and took a bite of an apple. It was so sweet. Why fruit tasted better in South Carolina than it ever had at home was a mystery. But in a way, it made sense, since life in general seemed so much better since she'd arrived in Magnolia Harbor.

"What are your plans tonight?" she asked.

"Zach and Marlene are arriving this evening," he answered. "They won't be staying at the inn because there isn't enough room, but they want to meet me here and go out to dinner."

"And your parents?"

Jesse averted his eyes. "Zach said they're arriving tomorrow morning."

"You must be excited about seeing them after so long," Becca remarked.

He sipped his water and didn't respond.

She wished he would tell her what was wrong. Her heart ached for the vulnerability she saw in his closed posture. She'd help him if she could, but he wouldn't let her. As close as they had become in such a short time, he obviously wasn't ready to lower that particular wall between them.

Jesse shifted his position, stretching his long legs out in front of him. He grimaced as he flexed his knee. "I'm more nervous than excited. I haven't seen my parents in eight years. I'm not exactly sure what to expect. Hopefully, I'll be able to talk to them before a lot of people arrive. The last thing I want is an audience."

Alarm bells went off in her mind. If he had only gone off to the military like he'd told her, why would it matter if the reunion was private or public? Sure, there would be tears. One would expect that after such a long separation. No, there was something else that was responsible for separating Jesse and his parents. Something darker and more painful than mere distance.

"What are you doing tonight?" Jesse asked.

"I need to work on my master's project," Becca said. "I've been having so much fun that I've gotten behind."

"You'll be able to get back on track, won't you?" Jesse asked, his voice warm with concern.

"I have plenty of time to complete the project," she assured him. "I'm more worried about you. Is there anything I can do to help?"

Jesse glanced away. "I've really enjoyed getting to know you. I can't remember ever feeling this relaxed in someone else's company."

Becca suddenly felt sick. He was about to tell her that he no longer wanted to see her. "I feel the same way about you," she said, bracing herself for yet another rejection.

He took a deep breath and met her eyes. "Actually, I would love it if you would come and meet my brother and sister tonight."

Becca was so stunned and confused that she couldn't speak. Why was she overreacting and jumping to conclusions? She frowned. If she wasn't feeling so betrayed by David and Chelsea, then she probably wouldn't be acting this upset and emotional right now.

"I know it might seem awkward, and it's a big favor," Jesse continued, "but I could really use a friend beside me."

Becca realized that he wanted her to provide moral support for him, as she had asked him to support her. She smiled, feeling like she was back on solid ground again. "Yes, I'll be there."

"Great," he said, then paused. "Will you go to the party with me too?"

She blinked.

"You don't have to," Jesse said quickly. "I was only thinking—"

"Of course I'll go," Becca said, interrupting him. "As long as your family doesn't mind."

Relief washed over his face. "They won't mind. It's a party, right?"

"How big is the party?" she asked.

"About fifty people are coming."

Becca realized that she hadn't brought anything to wear. When she'd packed for this trip, she hadn't expected to be attending a party. "I need to buy a new dress."

"No, you don't," Jesse said. "You always look gorgeous."

She felt her face flush, and she couldn't hold back a smile. "Thank you."

Before Jesse could say anything else, his phone pinged. He pulled it out of his pocket and unlocked it, then read the text. Without glancing at Becca, he reached over and grabbed her hand. She didn't think he was even aware that he did it.

"It's Marlene," he informed her as he tapped out a response. "She expects to be here within the hour." He squeezed her hand.

Becca wondered if he realized how tightly he was holding her hand. Somehow she doubted it. "We should go." She gently pulled her hand away, then threw the garbage into a bag and put the remaining food in the basket.

"Yeah, I need to shower and shave before they get here." Jesse practically jumped off the bench. Stress, nervousness, and excitement swirled around him.

"Absolutely." She touched his arm. "It's going to be fine, and I'll be right by your side."

He gave her a sheepish look. "Sorry. Guess I'm a bit on edge at the moment. Are you sure you don't mind coming and helping me survive my crazy family?"

"I don't mind at all." Becca snorted. "I think it'll be a whole lot stranger for you to attend the wedding of my cousin and ex-fiancé."

Jesse laughed. "When you put it like that, I see your point."

"I thought you would."

They returned to the inn and dropped off the basket in the kitchen. Jesse saw Becca to her room, then headed to his suite on the third floor.

Once Becca was alone, she found that some of Jesse's nervousness had transferred to her. What if his family didn't like her?

Walking over to the mirror, she examined her reflection. Nothing was wrong with her appearance. Granted, she wasn't nearly as beautiful as her sisters were, but she was pretty enough. She smiled as she remembered Jesse saying she was gorgeous. Maybe he was only being polite, but the compliment warmed her anyway.

The fact that Jesse had invited her would probably be enough for his family to accept her presence at least for one day. He said there would be about fifty people at the party. One more person wouldn't make that much of a difference.

Becca decided to go into town tomorrow to buy a new dress, despite what Jesse had said. But what about tonight? She had no idea what to wear.

Rummaging through her clothes, she found a pair of dress pants and a nice blouse. That should work. She could add a necklace and earrings to dress it up.

Becca dressed with care. Surveying her reflection again, she still wasn't sure. It would be helpful to get another woman's opinion.

She walked into the bathroom she shared with Leslie and knocked on the door to Leslie's suite.

There was no response.

Biting her lip, Becca pondered what she should do. She probably looked fine, but she wasn't always current on what was considered fashionable. Maybe she'd search for Grace or Charlotte. They both had impeccable taste in clothes, and they would certainly be a better judge than Becca. It couldn't hurt to see if they were downstairs.

Becca slipped out the door and descended the stairs. As she reached the bottom of the staircase, she heard voices. She inched forward hesitantly and saw Jesse talking to a man and a woman. The family resemblance was strong, and Becca immediately knew they were Jesse's siblings, Marlene and Zach.

Winston ran over to the family, obviously eager for their attention.

Marlene laughed, wiped the tears from her eyes, and patted the dog's head.

Winston wagged his tail and yipped.

When Jesse and Marlene embraced, Becca felt like an intruder, but she was glued to the spot.

"My turn," Zach said. "Move over."

Laughing, Marlene released Jesse.

Zach stepped in to take her place. "Good to see you."

Jesse and Zach hugged and pounded each other on the back.

Becca's eyes welled up with tears. Jesse had been so worried about seeing his family, but there was no evidence of any hard feelings from either of his siblings. In fact, they both seemed overjoyed to be with him again.

As Jesse stepped back, he glanced over and noticed Becca. If his smile was anything to go by, he definitely approved of what he saw. He headed toward her.

The front door opened, and someone yelled, "Jesse!"

Jesse's steps faltered, and he spun around.

A young blonde woman rushed over to Jesse and threw her arms around him.

Stunned, Becca scrambled for a logical explanation. Maybe this woman was Jesse's cousin.

The thought was quickly squashed when the young woman kissed Jesse on the lips.

Jesse pulled away from her. "Sarah, what are you doing here?"

Sarah pouted. "What do you mean? Didn't I tell you that I'd wait for you?"

Becca's world came crashing down around her. Again. Jesse already had a girlfriend. And one who had apparently waited for him for years.

Devastated, Becca whirled around and ran up the stairs.

"Becca, wait!" Jesse called.

But she wouldn't wait. She'd been the fool for the last time.

16

Jesse

Jesse was nearly snarling with frustration and irritation as he faced Sarah.

She smirked, a malicious glint in her eyes. "Who was that? Some poor country girl you've been playing with?"

Jesse wondered if he'd ever thought he loved Sarah. Maybe when he was young. Once he'd realized how cruel and petty she could be, he had immediately ended their relationship. It was too bad she hadn't gotten the message.

Ignoring Sarah, Jesse focused on his siblings. "Why is she here? You know we broke up years ago. I haven't talked to her since I left for boot camp."

"That's not what she told us," Marlene said, glaring at Sarah. "When it became common knowledge that you were discharged, she claimed you wanted to reconcile with her. We thought you'd be anxious to see her, so we brought her with us to surprise you."

"I made it clear that I wanted nothing to do with her a long time ago." Jesse crossed his arms over his chest. "And I haven't changed my mind."

"You don't know what you're saying," Sarah insisted. "You and I were always the perfect couple. We could be again." She rested her hand on his arm. "I've never stopped loving you."

Jesse yanked his arm away. He refused to have anything to do with Sarah. He'd seen her true colors. She was more than willing to lie and hurt others in order to get her own way. Sarah had even spread nasty rumors about other girls who had run against her for prom queen their senior year.

And now she had misled his family and hurt Becca, a good, kind, wonderful woman he could see himself falling in love with.

He was pretty sure he had already begun.

Becca had been deeply betrayed by a man. Jesse cringed when he pictured the wounded look in her eyes before she retreated to her room. He needed to talk to her, but he didn't feel right about abandoning his brother and sister so soon after they'd arrived.

Marlene seemed to read his thoughts, because she put her arm around his shoulders and said, "Go talk to Becca. Zach and I will take a tour of the grounds."

"Are you sure you don't mind?" Jesse asked them.

"Of course not," Marlene said.

"I could use some exercise," Zach added.

Jesse raced up the stairs, so intent on seeing Becca that he ignored the twinges in his knee. He stopped at her door and knocked.

No answer.

He knew she was in there, so he called out, "Becca, she's not my girlfriend. Please open the door."

Still no answer.

Maybe she was in the bathroom and didn't hear him. It was unlikely but still a possibility. Jesse pulled out his phone and sent her a text. *It's not what you think. I didn't betray your trust. She's not my girlfriend. Please talk to me.*

Becca didn't respond to the message or open the door.

Jesse didn't want to leave without explaining to Becca, but he needed to return to his siblings. He wouldn't give up, though. This was way too important to him. "I'll be back," he promised, then rushed downstairs.

Marlene and Zach walked through the front door.

"Where's Sarah?" Jesse asked.

"She called a cab," Zach replied. "I can't believe we fell for her story."

"All you had to do was ask me if we were together," Jesse said.

Marlene raised a hand. "It wasn't Zach's fault. It's on me. I thought we could surprise you. I wanted to see you happy. It must have been the romantic in me that wanted to believe you'd found love and that your life wasn't all pain and isolation. I had no idea you might have found someone else."

Jesse felt his anger melt. "There was hardship, but I actually enjoyed having a military career. Please don't feel bad for me."

"You're my baby brother," Marlene said with a grin. "It's my job to feel bad for you and fuss over you and be concerned when your life is difficult."

He chuckled, but he couldn't stop wondering about Becca. He hoped she'd allow him to explain.

"I'm starving," Zach said. "Let's grab a bite to eat."

"Where should we go?" Marlene asked.

Jesse searched restaurants on his phone. "Turner's Lakeside Grill sounds good. It's supposed to have amazing steak and seafood."

"I'm sold," Zach said.

They walked out to Zach and Marlene's rental car. When Zach got behind the wheel, Jesse gave him directions.

"So, who was she?" Zach asked as they drove. "She must be important."

"Becca Hart," Jesse replied. "I met her here, and she's really special to me."

"Did you explain to her what happened?" Marlene asked.

"I tried to, but she wouldn't answer the door when I knocked or respond to my text," Jesse said. "I'm afraid she's written me off after the stunt Sarah pulled. I doubt Becca will ever speak to me again."

Zach frowned. "It was irritating, but why wouldn't Becca talk to you? You didn't kiss Sarah back. Do you want us to tell Becca that you didn't know Sarah was coming and wouldn't have wanted her to?"

Jesse shook his head. "It's complicated, and it's not my place to tell her story."

"I'll respect your privacy, but I'm here if you need me," Zach said. "You know that, right?"

Jesse's throat closed. He knew it now. "Thank you," he managed to say quietly.

He wished that Becca were here with him. At first, Jesse had asked Becca to come along this evening for moral support. But now that he was with his brother and sister and no longer dreaded their reaction to him, he realized he wanted Becca here because of who she was becoming to him.

Now she wasn't even speaking to him.

Jesse had to try to talk to her again when he returned to the inn. He had to see if he could make her understand. He wouldn't give her up that easily.

He needed to tell her the whole story. She had told him her history, even the painful parts, and he owed her that much in return. He had to let her know the real reason he'd held back from seeing his parents until now. Including the final event that had convinced him to join the military and how he had done it.

Jesse wasn't looking forward to that conversation. Of course, if Becca still refused to speak to him, that conversation would never happen. And that would be even worse.

Another thought popped into his head. Did she still want him to pose as her fiancé at her cousin's wedding? He'd gotten used to the idea. At times he'd imagined what it would be like to truly be engaged to a woman as incredible as Becca.

Now he may not even be able to count her as a friend. All because of a stupid misunderstanding.

All because of Sarah.

Jesse forced himself to stop this train of thought. It was frustrating and getting him nowhere.

They arrived at Turner's Lakeside Grill. It was busy, but they were able to get a table.

Jesse, Marlene, and Zach seemed to pick up right where they'd left off as they caught up and shared stories and laughter. They'd been close growing up, and Jesse could feel their bond once again.

As they lingered over dinner, Jesse smiled. Being with his brother and sister and making them laugh was a healing experience for him. He would never let himself be emotionally separated from them again.

He still had to deal with his mom and dad, though. He prayed that they would accept him. Reconnecting with Marlene and Zach tonight had given him hope, but a sliver of doubt still lingered in his heart.

It was almost nine when Marlene and Zach dropped Jesse off at the inn. Even though it was a little late, Jesse was determined to see Becca. He approached the door to her suite and knocked gently.

She opened the door.

Jesse felt a deep sense of relief until he noticed the suitcase on her bed. "You're leaving?"

"I have no reason to stay."

Her flat answer devastated him. "Please let me talk to you for a few minutes."

Becca studied him. "Fine." She opened the door wider and stepped back.

As Jesse entered the room, he felt like he was walking on glass. Each move could destroy the fragile thread of hope she'd offered him. He perched on the edge of a stuffed armchair.

Becca sat on the bed. "What do you want to tell me?"

"Okay, first, I know what you're thinking," he said. "But I had no idea Sarah would be here. We broke up years ago, and I have absolutely no plans to reconcile with her. She lied to my siblings to get them to bring her here."

She nodded. "I knew I was overreacting the moment I ran off."

"Then why didn't you answer the door earlier?" he asked. "Or my text?"

"I wasn't ready to talk yet. I needed time to process things," Becca explained. "I turned my phone off so I wouldn't see any messages." She stared down at her feet. "I realized something tonight."

Jesse had a sinking feeling in his stomach.

"I have a bad habit of avoiding situations," she continued. "I also rely on others too much. I don't even know you that well, but I know you've been keeping a secret from me. I can see it in your face whenever we talk about your past. But I let myself become emotionally invested in you anyway. That's not smart."

He didn't respond.

"I need you to be honest with me," Becca said, finally meeting his eyes. "I think it's time you told me what really happened before you left. I've shared my burdens, and it's only fair that you share yours."

Jesse sucked in a deep breath for strength and courage. "You're right. I've wanted to tell you so many times, but it isn't easy to admit how much of an idiot I was."

"It can't be that bad," she said.

"You'd be surprised."

She raised an eyebrow at him. "Try me."

"Okay," he said. "My mom kept a scrapbook for each of us and meticulously recorded everything we did, including newspaper clippings and all our awards."

"It's nice that she saved those things," Becca commented.

"I already mentioned that my brother and sister were the shining stars of the family. They made the honor roll every single grading period." Jesse couldn't sit still anymore. He stood up, shoved his hands into his pockets, and began to pace in front of her, ignoring his knee. "I never made the honor roll. Not once. I wasn't flunking or anything, but I wasn't as good as they were."

She gave no outward reaction, but he could sense by her absolute stillness that she was attuned to his every word.

"My parents and teachers constantly begged me to be more like Marlene and Zach," Jesse went on. "If only I studied like my sister or took my classes more seriously like my brother. My dad was especially harsh. Maybe I could have done better, but the endless nagging got old real fast. By the time I was in high school, I was completely sick of it, and all I wanted to do was get out of there. At one point, I even threatened to drop out of school."

"That's terrible," Becca said.

"When I was a senior, I met Haley, and she became my reason for breathing. I was thrilled that she agreed to go out with me. She was always on the honor roll, but she never pressured me. Even so, I nearly made it on the honor roll that year."

"It sounds like things finally started getting better."

"They did," he said. "I took the ASVAB test for the military and scored high on it. I mean, really high. I was excited when I began receiving calls and literature from all the branches. My parents were pleased with my test score, but they tried to discourage my interest in the military."

Becca remained silent. No matter how deeply he searched her eyes, he couldn't figure out what she was thinking.

"Then something horrible happened." Jesse squeezed his eyes shut as the awful memories flooded back. "Haley and I were going to a restaurant. I was supposed to drive her, but I was running late, so she said she'd meet me there. But she never showed up."

"What happened?"

He wiped the tears from his eyes. The guilt never eased. "She was hit by a drunk driver on the way there. I couldn't deal with it. I spiraled out of control the rest of the year. Completely gave up. I hated everyone. Especially myself."

"It wasn't your fault," she said softly.

"Haley wouldn't have been on that road at all if she wasn't coming to meet me." He collapsed on the chair again and ran his fingers through his hair. "I fell in with a bad crowd, including Sarah. My dad and I argued constantly. He yelled at me one night to stop ruining my life and be a man. I told him I didn't want to be a man if it meant being like him. I stormed out and stayed at a friend's house. My mom tracked me down and called in the middle of the night. She told me that my dad had suffered a massive heart attack."

Becca gasped.

"When I went to the hospital, the doctors weren't sure he'd live." Jesse paused to gain control of his emotions. He couldn't meet Becca's gaze. He didn't want to see what she thought of him now. "My mom said the heart attack was because of me."

Silence fell between them.

Becca got up and walked over to Jesse. Her face was streaked with tears.

He stood, and she wrapped her arms around him. He clung to her, not sure which one of them was trembling.

"That was the last time I saw them," Jesse whispered. "As soon as I graduated from high school, I joined the military."

"You're here now," Becca reminded him as she gently freed herself from his embrace. "And it'll be wonderful to reunite with them."

"That's the thing," Jesse responded. "They don't even know I'm attending the party. My brother and sister said our parents will be overjoyed to see me. But what if they take one look at me and tell me to leave?"

"They won't do that to you," she said. "You're their son, and they love you."

"What if they haven't forgiven me for my dad's heart attack?" he asked.

"It wasn't your fault," Becca assured him. "It was a horrible coincidence. But you weren't to blame. Your mom was upset when she said that. By now, she'll have realized it's not true."

"I know you're right, but it's hard to let myself believe it." Jesse appreciated her compassion and kind words. Becca was certainly special. He spontaneously took her hand and squeezed it.

Becca's eyes caught his, and he knew she felt the current humming between them. Somehow in the past few moments, they'd moved past the invisible line that separated friends from something deeper.

There was no going back now. And somehow, he wasn't afraid of that.

17

Leslie

When Leslie woke up on Saturday morning, she decided to skip breakfast and remain in her room. Yesterday she'd kept a low profile, still hoping that she wouldn't have to leave. But she couldn't put it off any longer. Leslie needed to get out of Magnolia Harbor today.

The inn was buzzing with activity. All she had to do was glance out her window to see Grace, Charlotte, Winnie, and a dozen or so servers and helpers rushing around.

At first, she was puzzled. Then she recalled that Jesse was here for his parents' anniversary party. It appeared that it would be a large gathering.

With all the confusion, Leslie hoped she'd be able to sneak out without anyone noticing. She needed to be positive and stay alert for an opportunity to flee.

A gentle knock on her door startled her from her thoughts.

Leslie crept warily to the door. She peeked through the peephole and saw Charlotte standing on the other side, holding a covered tray. Overcome with relief, Leslie opened the door.

"I hope I'm not disturbing you," Charlotte said.

"No, not at all." Leslie stepped back. "Please come in."

"I didn't see you at breakfast, so I thought you might be hungry," Charlotte said. "I brought you scrambled eggs, toast, yogurt, and orange juice." She held out the tray.

Touched, Leslie accepted it. "You didn't have to do that. I feel bad that you went to so much trouble for me. Especially when you're clearly busy getting ready for the party."

Charlotte laughed. "I couldn't let a fellow chef starve, could I?"

"I'm not a chef yet," Leslie reminded her. "Hopefully, I'll earn that title one day."

Charlotte beamed. "I have no doubt you'll get there."

"Thank you," Leslie said, feeling her face flush. "That means a lot, coming from you."

"I'd better get back to work," Charlotte said. "Let me know if you need anything else."

After Charlotte left, Leslie took a seat and scarfed down her breakfast so fast that she barely even tasted it, though she did notice that Charlotte put a special seasoning in her eggs. She wished she had time to ask what it was. She pushed the tray aside and glanced around the room.

It would be too obvious if she took her whole suitcase with her, and she didn't want to risk getting caught. After dumping all her belongings on the bed, she rummaged through them. Leslie shoved only the most necessary items into her purse and backpack, then switched off her cell phone and slipped it into her purse. She left the rest of her things on the bed. There was no need to put them away. Maybe Grace and Charlotte would donate them.

She slung her purse and backpack over her shoulders. For a second, Leslie considered climbing over the edge of the veranda, but she'd never make it without being seen. Not to mention she'd probably fall and break a bone.

She quietly crept out of the room and closed the door behind her. No one was in the hall, so she flew down the stairs. The reception desk was unoccupied, and she didn't see anyone else around. Now was her chance.

As Leslie went out the front door, she spotted two women wearing aprons heading her way. They were probably here to assist with the party. She hurried to the parking area, terrified of being chased by Sergeant Groves or Will.

By the time she arrived at her car, she was sweating, but it wasn't from physical exertion. She jumped into the driver's seat and tossed her backpack and purse onto the passenger side. She sat there for a moment, waiting for her heart to stop racing.

When Leslie calmed down, she wondered if she had eluded Sergeant Groves. For what felt like the millionth time, she questioned whether she was seeing danger where none existed.

No, it was already too late. Her course was set, and if she went back now, she'd constantly be glancing over her shoulder. She'd miss Becca, Grace, and Charlotte. But she'd write to them later to explain her sudden departure. Hopefully, sometime in the future she'd finally become the person she wanted to be and achieve her culinary goals.

Someday.

But first, Leslie needed to get to a safe place. A place where Will would never find her. Then she could stop wondering if anyone was following her.

She was tired of living that way.

Leslie jabbed the key into the ignition and started the car. She was so tense that her shoulders ached. She eased her car out of the space and slowly traveled down the long lane. She longed to punch the gas, but she knew speed would attract attention.

She tried to remain calm as she drove through Magnolia Harbor, reminding herself that no one was following her and that it would be all right. She needed to decide where to go next. Should she head north or south?

When Leslie spotted a gas station, she stopped. Leaving the car running, she ran inside and grabbed a map. She paid for it and returned to her car.

Though she wanted to scour the map to locate a place to hide out, the station was too busy. She couldn't stay here. So she drove to the grocery store next door and parked. Once again, she left the car running. Leslie hated to waste the fuel, but she also didn't want to lose the comfort of the air-conditioning blasting cold air. The outside temperature was well above eighty degrees. The short jaunt to get a map had made her perspire. The heat alone almost persuaded her to head north.

"Hello, Leslie."

She froze, horror shooting ice down her spine, and glanced in the rearview mirror.

Will sat up in the back seat.

She stifled a scream and fumbled for the door handle.

Will lunged forward and grabbed her wrist. "I wouldn't try to escape. If you do as I say, everything will be fine. Life can go back to normal."

Leslie couldn't believe this was happening. "How did you find me?"

He smirked. "I've always known you might run once you realized what was right under your nose. I had a tracking device put on your car. I can't have my girlfriend damaging my reputation. Especially not when a whole new political scene is opening up to me."

She glanced around the parking lot, hoping someone would appear.

"The cops around here seem to know about me, but that won't help you," Will said. "You've kept your head in the sand so long, they're bound to think you were an accessory. You know what that means, don't you?" He smiled. "It means if I go to jail, so do you."

Leslie was breathing hard and fast, as if she'd run a marathon at top speed. There was nothing overtly threatening in Will's smile, but she knew him. He was a man used to getting exactly what he wanted. He wasn't above kidnapping her if he had to.

She had never considered that he might have put a tracking device on her car. Who did that? It was like a scene from a cheesy police drama, one where the writers paid little attention to the reality of police work and went for shock value instead.

She was shocked all right. More than that, though, Leslie was surprised to find that her main emotion was anger, not fear.

She would have to bide her time and be observant. Take the first opportunity that presented itself so she could escape.

Leslie had just discovered her dreams. She wouldn't give them up without a fight.

Grace

Saturday morning, Grace stood at the reception desk, checking her last-minute notes for the anniversary party this afternoon. The florist had delivered the flowers, and the caterers were setting up the buffet tables. It was a beautiful day with clear skies. Everything seemed to be in order, and she was relieved.

The bell above the front door jingled, and a well-dressed couple in their early sixties entered.

"Welcome to the Magnolia Harbor Inn. I'm Grace Porter, one of the owners." She smiled. "You must be Tim and Debby McFarland."

Tim nodded. "Nice to meet you."

"Thanks again for hosting our party here," Debby said.

"We're honored," Grace said. "Please let us know if you need anything."

Winston barreled into the room and raced to greet the couple.

"That's Winston," Grace said. "He enjoys meeting new people."

"He's precious." Debby cooed over Winston and lavished attention on him. "I love dogs. We have two corgis at home."

"Very nice," Grace said. "Would you like a tour of the grounds? Everything is set up for the party."

"Thank you," Tim said, "but our family is supposed to meet us here any minute."

"We already took a quick look around, and everything is absolutely perfect," Debby added.

"I'm glad you think so," Grace said.

The front door opened, and a man and a woman rushed inside and hugged Tim and Debby.

"Have you met our son and daughter?" Debby asked Grace.

"I haven't had the pleasure yet," Grace said.

Debby introduced Grace to Marlene and Zach.

"It's wonderful to meet you both," Grace said. She wondered where Jesse was and why no one in his family mentioned him.

"I still can't believe we let you talk us into throwing such an elaborate party," Debby chided her kids, although she was smiling. "We really don't need a party. After all, we have an anniversary every year."

Marlene rolled her eyes. "Thirty-five years of marriage is a big deal. You and Dad deserve to celebrate."

"I agree," Tim said. "I'm amazed she's put up with me that long."

Debby laughed, but it died away on a sigh. "If only . . ."

"I know," Tim said, putting his arm around Debby's shoulders.

Marlene glanced at her brother. He nodded.

"Jesse's here," Marlene told her parents.

Both Tim and Debby stared at their daughter.

"Jesse contacted us recently and said that he was out of the Army," Marlene said. "He was wounded."

Debby gasped.

"He's all right," Zach assured her. "It wasn't a life-threatening injury. Anyway, when I told him about the party, he wanted to come."

Debby's eyes welled up, and a tear slipped down her cheek. She faced her husband. "Do you think he's forgiven me for what I said? I never truly blamed him."

Tim pulled his wife closer. "I know."

"I think he's worried that you haven't forgiven him," Zach told his mother. "We've tried to get him to call you or visit, but he's been resisting."

"Where is he now?" Tim asked.

"He went into town this morning to run one last errand," Marlene said. "He promised to be back in time for the party."

"That's wonderful news," Debby said, her voice shaking.

"I think we'll take you up on the tour of the grounds now," Tim said to Grace.

"Of course." Grace escorted the family outside and showed them around.

Winston accompanied the group, stopping once in a while to chase a butterfly.

Grace left the family to enjoy their time together. She and Winston returned to the inn.

A moment later, Mason burst through the front door. His face was pale.

Grace tensed. Something was wrong. Immediately, she grew concerned for the safety of her guests. "What's the matter?"

"Where's Leslie?" Mason asked. "I can't find her."

"I haven't seen her this morning," Grace said, trying not to panic. "Charlotte took a tray up to her earlier because she missed breakfast. But I haven't heard anything else. Perhaps she's still in her room."

"I doubt it," he said. "When I couldn't find her, I knocked on her door, and no one answered."

"Well, she might not have wanted company," she reasoned.

Mason shook his head. "I searched the grounds too. Her car is missing from the parking lot."

"Maybe she went to town," Grace suggested. She checked Leslie's reservation on the computer. "She hasn't checked out yet."

"I know this isn't normal procedure, but I need you to unlock Leslie's room and let me search it." Mason frowned. "Will Canfield was spotted in Magnolia Harbor very early this morning. He knows she's in town, and it's only a matter of time before he locates her."

Grace nodded and grabbed the extra key from behind the desk. "Let's go." She led Mason to Leslie's room and knocked on the door. "Leslie, are you in there? It's Grace, and I need to talk to you. It's urgent. Please open the door."

There was no response.

She didn't like opening Leslie's door and invading her privacy, but what did that matter compared to Leslie's safety? Sliding the key into the lock, Grace opened the door.

Mason burst into the room and searched it and the bathroom. "She's not here," he announced.

Grace walked over to the bed. "Her suitcase is still here," she murmured, hoping that meant Leslie planned to return.

"Her suitcase is here, but she's gone." He pointed at the bed. "Look at the mess she left."

She frowned. It was clear that Leslie had been going through her things in a haphazard manner. "That doesn't seem like Leslie."

"It's not," Mason said. "My profile on her says she's almost obsessively neat. It appears she was gathering only what she absolutely needed. Have you ever seen her with a smaller bag?"

Grace's heart sank. "Yes. I've seen her with a backpack. Not a large one."

"It makes sense," Mason said. "I think she was aware that I was following her. I'm afraid I was a little too sure of myself. It appears that she ran to get away from me as well as her ex."

"What do we do now?" Grace asked, wringing her hands.

He glanced around the room one last time. "I need to contact Captain Daley and ask the local police to start watching for Leslie's car. We need to find her. Before Canfield does."

19

Jesse

Jesse glanced at the bouquet he'd gotten for his mother. It wouldn't make up for all the stress and anguish he'd caused her, but it was all he had to give her.

He wasn't looking forward to the party. At the same time, he was anxious to see his parents again. He missed them. He missed his mom's gentle smile and the way she could always make him feel better. He missed watching games with his dad. Before they started fighting so much, they had been connected by their love of sports. No one else in the family understood their obsession with football and wrestling. And no one was prouder of him than his dad when Jesse had made it to the state competition his final year on the wrestling team.

Things had changed the last few months at home. Could he really go back?

No, things would never be the same again. Too much time had passed.

But right now, Jesse would settle for any type of relationship with his parents.

If they would forgive him. Forgive him for being irresponsible and selfish, for not thinking of them when he had started to get into trouble. He'd never once considered opening up to them about the darkness in his life.

His parents had known about Haley's death, but they hadn't understood how much she had meant to him. He'd all but hidden that relationship from them. Why? It seemed stupid now, but at the time he'd blatantly refused to share that part of his life with his family. And it had cost him.

His phone dinged, and he checked the screen.

It was a text from Becca. *Still want me to come to the party?*

Please, he wrote back. *Are you still okay with it?*

I promised, she replied.

Jesse wasn't quite sure what Becca meant by that, but at least she hadn't rejected him. Even after everything, she was still going to the party to support him. That had to be worth something. Soon he would return the favor. But now he felt weird about going to a wedding where he would pretend to be in love with a woman he was truly starting to fall for.

He shook his head. Now was not the time to broach the subject. He and Becca were still a bit too emotionally fragile for anything heavy like falling in love.

His phone pinged again. It was a text from his brother. *Mom and Dad are here. Marlene spilled the beans about you. It's all good.*

What's all good? he wrote back. Were their parents safe and happy to be here? Had they accepted his presence for the sake of peace? Maybe even forgiven him? Jesse hoped so. He wouldn't really know until he could look into his mother's eyes and see the expression in them.

Would she hug him and call him her baby again?

It used to drive him crazy when she did that in front of other people. Now he yearned for it with a soul-deep hunger. And until he'd talked with Becca last night, no one had hugged him in a long time.

Jesse was on an emotional roller coaster, and it terrified him. He had to keep it together, make it through today. Then he'd be able to decide what to do next.

He checked his phone, but Zach hadn't responded. It was almost noon, and time was slipping away from him. Jesse quickly took a shower and got dressed.

Grabbing the bouquet, he went down to the second floor. He stopped outside Becca's suite and knocked.

A moment later, Becca opened the door. She was dazzling in a jade-green dress and silver sandals. She'd left her hair hanging loose, and it spilled around her shoulders in red curls. When she smiled, her eyes sparkled behind her glasses.

She was the most beautiful woman he'd ever seen. Suddenly, his anxiety fled. He was proud she was allowing him to escort her to his parents' anniversary party. Hopefully, they would be welcoming to her. Even if they weren't pleased to see him.

Jesse swiftly put an end to his negative thoughts. Instead, he focused on the woman in front of him. "You're absolutely stunning."

"Really?" Becca asked. There was a lifetime of doubt in her voice.

Had no one ever told her how lovely she was? He recalled when she'd mentioned that her sisters were gorgeous, hinting that she was different. He'd wondered at the comment briefly then. Now, staring at her, he saw in her eyes the need to believe.

Jesse and Becca were both wounded souls, longing for acceptance.

The desire to protect her from further hurt or slights stirred inside him. But he didn't have that right. Maybe someday he'd be able to earn it. He really hoped so.

"Yes, truly. You're beautiful." He smiled and held out his arm. "Shall we go?"

She took his arm. "I'm ready."

They descended the stairs and made their way outside to the spacious lawn. The guests had already started to arrive, and Jesse ushered Becca over to the long line of people waiting for their turn to greet the guests of honor.

The older couple in front of them recognized Jesse as Tim and Debby's youngest child. He had a vague recollection of meeting them before.

"We were the best man and maid of honor at your parents' wedding," the woman reminded him.

"I heard you're in the military," the man said, shaking Jesse's hand. "Army, isn't it?"

"Yes, sir. I'm out now." Jesse didn't go into all the details. He was a little stunned to find out that his parents had talked about him. The couple in front of him were gracious, and it didn't seem as if they'd ever heard anything negative about him.

Maybe it was a sign that things would work out.

Without thinking about it, he reached over and took Becca's hand. She stilled. He considered letting go, but then she wrapped her fingers around his. Warmth spiraled through him.

Glancing around, Jesse was quite impressed with how nice the grounds looked today. He would never have guessed that only a few days earlier the yard had been torn up with deep ruts. The lawn care crew had outdone themselves.

Then he spotted his parents. They hadn't seen him yet. They were talking to each other and laughing.

Just then, his mom met his eyes and gasped. She clutched her husband's arm and shrieked.

The guests around them stopped talking and looked to see what the commotion was about.

His mom ran to Jesse and threw her arms around him.

He released Becca's hand to embrace his mother, ignoring the tears that streamed from his eyes. "I'm sorry, Mom," he whispered into her ear. "So sorry."

She was shaking, which meant she was weeping too. "No, I'm sorry.

My baby. Oh, Jesse, you're here. My baby is here."

Jesse squeezed his eyes shut. His heart was too full for words.

His mother gently released him.

When Jesse opened his eyes, he saw his father. He'd visibly aged in the past eight years. It was partly because of his heart attack, but Jesse knew that his absence had played a part in his dad's appearance as well. The older man's expression was unreadable.

Jesse stood there, unsure what to do. His dad wasn't a hugger. Jesse couldn't remember the last time he'd seen him hug anyone other than his wife.

Then his father walked over and embraced Jesse. "Welcome home. We've missed you."

Jesse was overwhelmed. He had feared that his parents would reject him. Instead, they'd welcomed him back with open arms.

His mom wrapped her arm around his waist. "I am so sorry that I hurt you."

"I'm sorry too." Jesse held her tightly again. "We all said things we shouldn't have." He scanned the crowd, noting that there were tears on many of the faces. "We seem to be causing a stir here."

His mom wiped her eyes. "I'm so glad I didn't put on mascara."

They all laughed.

Jesse saw that Becca was standing a few feet away. Her eyes were shiny, but she was smiling. She was also holding the flowers he'd brought for his mother. He had no memory of dropping them. He reached out and pulled her in. "Mom and Dad, I want you to meet my friend Becca Hart. She's my guest today."

Maybe someday he'd be able to introduce her as something more than a friend.

"It's lovely to meet you, my dear," his mom said. "How did you two meet?"

Becca's face flushed. She was probably thinking about her ex-fiancé and her cousin. Then she glanced at Jesse.

He was entranced by the sparkle in her hazel eyes. She took his breath away.

"I'm staying at the inn to work on my master's project," Becca explained to his mother. "I met your son this week, and we clicked." She cast another glance at Jesse. This one was definitely flirtatious. "I have to admit, I haven't gotten nearly as much done on my project as I thought I would."

Jesse grinned at Becca, enjoying her playful attitude. "We'll let you greet the rest of your guests," he told his parents. "I'll talk to you in a little bit."

"I'm so afraid you'll disappear again," his mom said quietly.

He met her gaze. "I'm not going anywhere ever again."

His parents hugged him, then moved to greet their other guests.

Jesse ushered Becca around, introducing her to the people he knew. When he got to Marlene and Zach, he gladly endured another round of hugs.

"I told you it would be okay, didn't I?" Zach grinned. "I was right. You were worried about nothing."

"Yeah, yeah," Jesse said. "You were right." He punched his brother playfully on the arm.

Zach winced. "Still a slugger, aren't you?"

Even recovering from his wounds, Jesse was stronger than his older brother. It hadn't occurred to him as a kid that he was more athletically gifted than his siblings. Now he considered the fact that while their scrapbooks were filled with scholarly awards and accolades, his wasn't empty. His was filled with pictures of him winning medals and articles about the sports events he had participated in. In their own way, his parents had been proud of him too. But Jesse had been too blind to see it.

"I don't know about anyone else, but I'm starving," Jesse announced.

"Let's get something to eat," Zach said.

The foursome descended on the buffet tables, filled their plates, and sat down together.

Jesse had a great time talking and laughing with Becca and his siblings. He glanced over at his parents and was heartened to see the joy on their faces as they chatted with relatives and old friends. He was so glad to be here.

As the party started to wind down, Jesse stood with his family to say goodbye to the guests and thank them for attending.

Jesse noticed Becca standing off to the side and waved to get her attention.

She smiled at him.

He walked over to her and noticed a faraway look in her eyes. "Are you doing all right?"

"I'm fine," she said. "But it's time for me to leave."

"Please stay a little longer," he said.

"You need to enjoy the time you have with them," Becca said, motioning to his family. "I'm so happy that you reconciled."

Jesse was torn. He wanted to return to his family, but he also wanted to spend more time with her.

Becca didn't wait for him to respond, and he felt a small hole in his heart as he watched her walk away.

"I like your girlfriend," his mother murmured as she joined him.

"I like her too." He kissed her temple. "But she's not my girlfriend."

She smiled. "You want her to be." It wasn't a question.

"Yeah, I want her to be my girlfriend," Jesse admitted. "Maybe more someday."

Now he just had to find a way to convince Becca.

20

Becca

Becca hung the green dress in the closet with care, running her hands lovingly over the silky fabric. She'd been surprised to find such a gorgeous piece that fit her so well at Miss Millie's. She was glad she'd purchased it, because she'd never forget the look in Jesse's eyes when he first saw her in it. Never in her life had she felt so beautiful.

Now she was back to ordinary Becca in her jean shorts and T-shirt.

Reluctantly, she let go of the dress and closed the closet door. Her hair was still wet from her shower. She left it hanging around her shoulders and stepped into a pair of sandals. Grabbing her laptop and a bottle of water, she went outside to sit on the veranda.

As the warmth from the sun enveloped her, Becca leaned back in her chair and shut her eyes, leaving the laptop closed.

She had enjoyed herself at the anniversary party. It was fun spending time with Jesse and his siblings and meeting his parents. She couldn't have been happier for Jesse. He'd been so afraid that his parents would reject him, but they'd been kind and welcoming. It was a wonderful reunion.

She'd been touched by how both Jesse and his mother had publicly apologized for the hurtful words they'd said, words that had separated the family for years. They had both admitted their wrongdoing, allowing Jesse to release his regrets and live in the moment.

That was something Becca couldn't do yet because there was a lie standing between her and true peace. A lie that she had started, even though she had never meant for it to get so out of hand.

Lies had a way of doing that.

Pushing the gloomy thoughts away, Becca turned her mind to more positive memories. She smiled as she recalled how Jesse had taken her hand. It had felt so natural, and when he'd let go, she missed his hand holding hers. She was certain, more than ever, that she was falling for him. Given enough time, what they had could develop and flourish. It could even lead to a future together.

And Becca was terrified.

She'd given her heart to David, and it had only led to betrayal and pain. After experiencing such a devastating breakup, she didn't know if she was ready to risk that pain again.

David and Chelsea had smashed her heart in the most hurtful way, and she wasn't sure how to get past that. If she opened up to Jesse the way she wanted to, she would also be opening herself up to future heartbreaks.

Even if Jesse proved to be the man she believed he was and even if they had a wonderful marriage, it wouldn't last forever. Happily ever after was a myth. Invariably, one person would die before the other, leaving the other to move on alone. She'd seen that happen to her mother when her father had passed away. Her mom had been devastated.

Becca stood and walked to the railing. The garden and the spacious lawn were magnificent, but she didn't really see any of it.

She had come so close to telling Jesse that she thought she was falling for him, but fear and caution had stopped her. Once she said those words, she could never take them back.

Maybe a long walk would help to clear her head. She returned to her room and grabbed her key, then went downstairs to the foyer.

"There you are," a voice called out. "I have something for you."

Becca turned and saw Winnie approaching her. The older woman carried a book.

"I'm so glad I caught up with you," Winnie said. "I found this today and thought of you. I want you to have it." She pressed the book into Becca's hands. "It will help, I promise." Then she walked away.

Becca gaped after her.

Someone laughed softly.

Becca spun around to see Charlotte standing behind the reception desk. "What just happened?" she asked.

Charlotte laughed again. "Winnie happened. I know it sounds strange, but my aunt has a way of giving people what they need when they need it." She shrugged. "It's who she is."

Becca glanced down at the book. It appeared to be very old. She carefully opened the brown leather cover and scanned the first page that had yellowed with age. "This is Diana Mellow's journal." She frowned. "Who's Diana Mellow?"

"Your guess is as good as mine," Charlotte answered.

Curious, Becca flipped through the journal. "I think I'll check it out."

She waved to Charlotte and went to her room, where she settled into the chair on the veranda with the journal on her lap. She closed her eyes for a few minutes, savoring the summer day with all its scents, the sound of the birds, and the splashing of frogs jumping in the lake.

Eventually, the weight of the journal on her lap begged her to open it. She ran her fingers over the smooth leather cover. There was something comforting about old books. She had always had a healthy reverence for the written word. As much as she loved her e-reader, print was always her favorite medium when reading for pleasure.

Opening to the first page of the journal, she noted that Diana Mellow had lovely penmanship, flowing and feminine. The initial entry was nearly seventy years ago when Diana had been a young woman of twenty.

Running her fingers along the top of the pages, Becca was surprised when she felt a small, thin protrusion. There was a bookmark in the journal. Not a piece of ribbon that was part of the journal itself but a cardstock bookmark.

How odd.

Opening the page to the bookmark, Becca began to read.

Today was Daniel's funeral. I stood in the crowd, watching his brothers and sister drop flowers into his grave. I tried not to weep. What right did I have to cry? I had turned him away when he had offered me his heart so many years ago. I'd had too many grand plans to see the world, and Daniel, my sweet Daniel, would have tied me down. Or so I believed.

All my lonely travels felt empty. I came home older and wiser to find that Daniel was no longer the strong and healthy man I had denied. My sister, Emma, told me that I had been spared the trouble of nursing someone while I was still young and beautiful. How could she understand the pain such words caused me? To be there and ease his suffering, to bring him comfort—such joy that would have been!

Instead, Daniel had nurses. For he had kept his promise to me and had never married. He had promised that his heart would remain mine for the rest of his life.

And now he is gone. I will always mourn him, without the memories of joyful times to ease my grief.

How foolish and vain I was to think I could ever find anything better than him in the world. I would gladly give up every adventure I ever had, if only I could have a week to bask in his love and let him know that he had mine as well.

Becca flipped to the last journal entry that had been written two years later. The tone was bitter, and she wondered if Diana had ever married.

Becca picked up her phone and searched for Diana Mellow from Magnolia Harbor, South Carolina. She came across an obituary notice for a seventy-four-year-old woman, still living in the town she grew up in. Her survivors listed a sister, Emma, and multiple nieces and nephews. There was no mention of a husband preceding her in death.

So Diana had never married. Had she grieved Daniel until she died?

Becca felt as if she couldn't breathe. What a tragedy. Diana had lived her life without ever really knowing love. Yet all the while she'd known that such a love had been right before her eyes, and she had tossed it away like garbage.

Becca jumped to her feet, unable to remain sitting. She snatched up the journal and strode into her room. She had so many things to do.

She wanted to have a chance with Jesse. If he still wanted her.

She stopped as the lie they were perpetuating smacked her in the face. How could she expect anything good and lasting to come from such deceit? That was what had really hurt her about David and Chelsea—the fact that two people she had thought loved her had lied to her.

Wasn't she doing the same thing?

Except it was worse because she was involving Jesse in her lie. It was true that he had offered to play the role of her fiancé. And maybe that was wrong of him, although she was more inclined to believe that he had truly wanted to help her.

Jesse didn't seem like a person who lied. Even his omission of the story involving his parents had not been a lie. He had simply kept the story private. It hadn't been her right to know everything, and his not telling her hadn't really hurt her.

But if Becca let him act out a lie with her, it would taint their whole relationship, the same way it was affecting her relationship with her family right now. She had not spoken to her sisters since she left, nor had she answered any of their texts. She'd never done that before. If it hadn't been for the whopper of a lie she'd told, she would be talking to them, letting them comfort her and commiserate with her.

Becca suddenly realized that she missed her sisters and her emotionally distant mother. She missed them all.

She would fix this. She had to. If she wanted any kind of relationship going forward with either Jesse or her family, it needed to be grounded in truth.

Sitting on the bed, she reached for her phone. With trembling fingers, she dialed Veronica's number.

Veronica answered on the second ring. "We've been so worried about you. Where are you? Are you all right? Did you get hurt?"

The flurry of questions hurtled at her convinced Becca that what she had done had been selfish. Not one of her sister's questions dealt with David or Chelsea. Every one of them was centered around the fact that the family was worried about her well-being. Becca was loved. She was blessed.

"I'm fine," Becca assured her. "I'm sorry that I was so selfish. Forgive me for not staying in touch with you or anyone else."

"You needed to get away to process your feelings," Veronica said. "I don't care as long as you're all right. Let's do a video chat so we can catch up. We'd feel better if we could see you." She disconnected without waiting for Becca to respond.

Thirty seconds later, the notification for a video chat popped up on her screen.

Becca answered the call and found herself staring at both her sisters and her mother. "I didn't know you were all there."

"Rebecca Ann," her mother began.

Becca knew she was in trouble whenever her mother used her middle name. Well, she definitely deserved it this time.

"Where have you been?" her mother scolded. "We've been worried sick. All we knew was that you were going somewhere to work on your master's project. No phone calls, no e-mails, no texts."

"You could have at least responded to one of my texts, so that we knew you were all right," Victoria added.

Underneath her sister's frown, Becca could see her love and compassion. Ashamed, she blinked back tears. "I'm sorry. I was so hurt when I got the wedding invitation from Chelsea that I didn't even think of you guys. All I could think of was that my fiancé had cheated on me with my own cousin."

"I thought that's what it was," her mother said. "Honestly, you're better off without him."

Becca gaped at her mother. "But I thought you liked David. You were always bragging about how your daughter was going to marry a doctor."

Her mom rolled her eyes. "Well, of course I did. I might not have liked him, but I love you and he was your choice. My bragging was for you. I'm sorry he hurt you, but I'm so relieved that he won't be my son-in-law."

Becca was stunned.

"So, about this new fiancé," Veronica said with clear trepidation. "You haven't done anything foolish, have you?"

"Yes and no," Becca admitted.

They all gasped.

"No, I'm not engaged," Becca said. "I was foolish enough to fill out that RSVP when I was feeling spiteful. I wasn't going to mail it, but someone found it and did it for me."

"Thank goodness you're not actually engaged again," Victoria said in obvious relief.

"I have met someone on this trip, though," Becca told them. "Someone I really like. He offered to help me save face by pretending to be my fiancé at the wedding, but I'm not going to let him do that. I don't want to have a lie standing in our way."

Her mom nodded. "I've always known that you're intelligent and have a lot of integrity. I might not say it often, but I am proud of you. Very proud."

"Thank you," Becca whispered. She had waited a long time to hear her mother say that. Tears blurred her eyes, and she wiped them away.

"Enough of this mushy stuff," Victoria said imperiously. "Tell us about this new guy."

As Becca filled them in, she realized that she couldn't wait to introduce Jesse to them. She was sure they would love him as much as she did.

Wait . . . love? Am I ready for that?

But even as she wondered about it, she knew that whether she was ready or not, it had already happened.

"We'd better let you go," her mother said. "Enjoy the rest of your time there. We can't wait until you get home."

When the call ended, Becca knew there was no going back. Now she had to talk with Jesse. The conversation wouldn't be easy, but it had to be done.

For the sake of their future.

21

Leslie

Leslie was terrified as Will forced her to drive away from the grocery store. But as she drove, she grew angry. What was she doing, allowing him to control her again?

An hour outside of Magnolia Harbor, her car got a flat tire, and she didn't have a jack or a spare.

They were stranded, so they got out and walked. Leslie watched for a chance to escape, but Will gripped her arm. Besides, there was nowhere to run anyway.

They trudged along until he found a car to steal and forced her to get in and drive.

Soon they needed to stop for fuel, and Will directed her to a gas station. "Stay here while I pump the gas."

While Leslie waited, her mind spun with ideas for escape. If she were braver, she'd get out and run, but he'd overtake her in a minute. And she was afraid that other people might get in the way. She wasn't willing to risk anyone else's safety.

Will jumped into the passenger seat. "Let's go."

"I won't drive you anywhere else," Leslie announced, crossing her arms over her chest. Since she was sitting in the driver's seat, he'd have to force her out of the car if he wanted to drive.

She was done. Completely done. Who did he think he was? She was no longer the naive woman he'd dated. Or rather used. She was a grown woman, and she would no longer be a victim. She had hopes and dreams now, a path to become the kind of person she wanted to be.

There was no way she would give that up.

A quiet voice in her mind warned her not to test his temper, but she immediately discarded that idea. Will was a crook, and he was conceited and coldhearted. One thing he was not, however, was violent. He was capable of violence, but she'd never seen him hurt anyone. She didn't think he was that far gone yet.

The worst she had ever seen him do was yell. Well, he could yell all he wanted.

Leslie was sitting in a stolen car in a public gas station parking lot. If Will tried to do anything or attempted to force her to drive the car anywhere, there were plenty of witnesses. She decided it was better to face him here than deal with him in some out-of-the-way place where she had no chance of getting help. Scanning the parking lot, she could see that they had already garnered some attention. Two older ladies were watching them closely.

"You're making this much more difficult than it has to be," he said.

She refused to respond.

"I don't want to have this conversation here." Will smiled at her, the charming smile he always used to convince her that he could be trusted. "Sweetheart, I know you heard something on the phone that worried you, but I promise you it was only a misunderstanding. Come on. Let's go home. We can talk about it on the way. It was all a mistake. You'll see."

"No," Leslie said. "And you can cut the act. It's not going to work. I refuse to go anywhere with you. I will not let you use me or my family's good name to further your crimes any longer." She glared at him. "We're done."

Will clenched his fist.

Her pulse pounded in her ears, and she pressed herself against the seat, realizing too late that she'd pushed him too far.

"You'll do what I say if you know what's good for you," he snarled in her face.

Suddenly, her confidence that he would never hurt her was gone. She'd never seen him get violent, but she'd also never seen anyone cross him as she was doing now.

It made Leslie more determined not to give in. She lifted her chin and glared her defiance at him, folding her arms over her chest. If she went with him, her freedom would be gone. Her bright future would be shattered.

"Will Canfield, put your hands behind your head and get out of the car," someone barked.

He swore and let go of her.

Leslie whirled around. A police car was stationed directly behind them. Sergeant Mason Groves was poised a few feet outside the car, gun pointed at Will. More police cars surrounded them, and an ambulance was parked off to the side. Leslie noticed the two older women who had been watching them a few minutes ago talking to a police officer.

They must have recognized a dangerous situation and called for help. They had probably saved her life.

A shudder ran through Leslie, and she felt faint. Until she'd seen the police, she hadn't realized how frightened she was. The fear was setting in now. Will had kidnapped her. He had tried to force her to go home with him.

She couldn't stop the tears that filled her eyes. She dashed them away, irritated with herself. She didn't need to be scared anymore. She was safe now.

Will didn't move, but she could see the muscles bunched up in his jaw. He looked like he was ready to burst into a rage, but his expression revealed that he knew he was cornered.

Leslie was frightened of what Will's desperation might make him do. She couldn't stand the idea of sitting in this car with him for one second longer. Without thinking about it, she threw open her door and fell to the ground beside the car as he made a grab for her. Will's hand brushed her hair, and she scrambled away.

"Get out of there," someone called out. "Go to the captain."

The captain raised his hand and gestured for her to move.

She ran to his side.

"Don't worry, Ms. Thomas," the captain said. "You're safe now. We're not going to let anything happen to you."

Nausea swirled in her stomach. Leslie sucked in two slow, deep breaths, trying to calm down.

Will refused to leave the car.

As she watched the standoff, she hugged herself and shivered, her teeth chattering. It was eighty degrees in the shade, but she was freezing.

A young paramedic draped a blanket over her shoulders. "You're going into shock. Let's get you warmed up."

"I can't be going into shock," Leslie argued, her voice sounding far away even to her own ears. "I'm not hurt."

"Emotional trauma can cause it too," the paramedic said. "Please let me help you."

She allowed the paramedic to usher her over to the ambulance and help her sit down on a stretcher. He asked her a steady stream of questions.

Her mind was a little fuzzy, but she was aware that the paramedic was trying to find out if she was disoriented.

"Why don't you lie down?" the paramedic asked gently. "I want to get your feet elevated."

Leslie allowed him to help her recline on the stretcher, but then she started to panic. "I can't see Will. I need to see him. I have to know where he is, or he'll sneak up on me again." She struggled to a sitting position.

"Please stay still and lie back," the paramedic urged. "Everything is going to be fine. The police won't let him anywhere near you."

Mason and another police officer finally dragged Will out of the vehicle.

Will yelled and fought, but he was unable to break free.

Mason pinned him to the car. Will's face was red, but Mason wasn't even breathing hard.

Leslie vaguely marveled at how strong the officer was.

Mason read Will his rights, then handed him off to the other officer, who hauled him to a police car.

Leslie watched with dry eyes as the car sped away, taking Will out of her life.

Mason came over to her. "Are you all right?" he asked gently.

Leslie didn't respond. She glanced at the car she'd been in, then back at Mason. It took a few seconds, but it finally sank in.

She was safe. She was free.

Leslie smiled at Mason. Then she fainted.

Grace

Grace smiled as she watched Jesse and his family sitting at a table together under the tent. She'd gotten the impression that there might have been some tension between Jesse and his parents, but the bonds of love that held the family together were obvious, even to an outsider like herself.

Winston stood at attention by her side, watching the family too. No doubt he wanted to romp over to them and see if they wanted to play, but he seemed to sense that now was not the time. That didn't stop him from watching and hoping, though. The little dog whined softly.

Grace patted his furry head. "I know, but it's best if we don't disturb them."

He gazed at her, his eyes pleading.

"I'm sorry," she told him. "They'll play with you later."

Grace glanced around. Most of the guests had already left the party. She realized that she hadn't noticed Becca leave, but the young woman was nowhere to be seen. She shrugged. Most likely, Becca had left to allow the family to have some time to themselves.

She walked away to give the family their privacy. She had plenty of other things that needed to be done. It wouldn't hurt if she waited another hour to tidy the area. Grace had offered to clean up and insisted that Charlotte go home to her cottage and relax. Because of the party, they'd canceled their usual hospitality hour.

Winston trotted behind her, his claws clicking on the pavement. Seeing the family together, Grace missed her own son. She had been so busy this week that she'd hardly had a chance to talk to Jake. She would have to call him this evening and see how things were in Raleigh, North Carolina. Jake was doing very well in his job as a software programmer, and she was proud of him.

As Grace walked around the inn to the front steps, she noticed Spencer exiting his car.

Pleasure bloomed inside her, but she quickly tamped it down.

Winston, however, was overjoyed to see Spencer. He bounded over to him and barked, begging for attention.

Chuckling, Spencer obliged the dog, then joined Grace at the foot of the stairs.

Grace greeted him, quite pleased with how calm she sounded. "Are you picking up Olivia? I haven't seen her today."

"Actually, I didn't come to see Olivia," Spencer said. "I came to see you."

"Oh, how nice." She gestured toward the inn. "Would you like to come inside?"

As they climbed the stairs, Grace glanced at Spencer out of the corner of her eye. He was a handsome man, and very little ever seemed to bother him. She wanted to ask him how serious things were between him and Olivia, but she knew that would not be a good thing to do. It was none of her business, and it would make things awkward between them.

Even more awkward than they'd been in the past week. No, longer than that. If she were being honest, things had been awkward between her and Spencer since she'd put the brakes on their budding relationship.

"How are things here?" he asked when they entered the foyer. "I ran into the captain today, and he mentioned that one of your guests had gone missing."

"I'm not sure I would exactly classify her as missing," Grace said.

"I believe Leslie left of her own free will. But the police are still keeping an eye out because there is some question about it."

"I'm sorry." He put a hand on her arm. "I know how much you care about your guests. Forgive me for not being around much this week. I haven't been a very good friend to you lately."

She almost winced when he said the word *friend*. Yes, she had wanted to be friends with him. However, now she wasn't certain that was all she wanted. But she couldn't say anything until she knew for sure what she wanted—and what he wanted. That was no longer clear either.

A lilting voice called Spencer's name. Olivia sashayed toward them. Her blonde hair was piled on top of her head, and she wore a white dress and gold bangle bracelets. Olivia minced up to Spencer in a thick cloud of perfume and gave him a kiss on both cheeks.

Winston backed away and tucked himself behind Grace's legs.

"Are you here to see me?" Olivia asked Spencer, fluttering her long lashes at him. "I was on my way out to dinner. Would you like to join me?"

Grace held her tongue with effort. It was obvious that Spencer had been talking to her. Although she was sure that Olivia meant no harm, she still felt the rudeness of the woman's interruption. She waited to see how Spencer would react.

"Actually, I'm here to see Grace," Spencer told Olivia. "Thank you for the kind offer. I hope you have a nice dinner."

Grace wanted to laugh out of the sheer joy that she would have Spencer's company to herself. It had been a while since he'd stopped by to see her.

"Oh." Olivia pouted, then gave Spencer another kiss on the cheek. "*Bien sûr, mon cher,*" she purred. "Another time." She walked away, blowing a kiss over her shoulder.

Grace glanced over, expecting to see Spencer watching Olivia flounce out the door. Instead, his gaze was fixed steadily on her. His eyes were warm, and his lips were curled in a slight smile. Her heart fluttered.

"I could use a snack," Grace remarked. "How about you?"

As if on cue, his stomach rumbled.

She laughed. "Let's go to the kitchen. I'm sure I can find us something to eat."

"I think raiding your refrigerator sounds fantastic," Spencer said.

Grace led him to the kitchen.

Winston followed, clearly hoping to be included in their informal dinner.

She peeked into the refrigerator and found leftover pasta with broccoli and plenty of fixings for a salad. "How about pasta and salad?"

"Sounds great," Spencer said. "What can I do?"

"You can get the plates and silverware." Grace slid the pan of pasta into the microwave. While it heated, she tore up lettuce leaves and added shredded carrots, croutons, walnuts, and cranberries, then drizzled the whole salad with Charlotte's special vinaigrette.

Spencer put two place settings on the large island. "What's next?"

She took the pasta out of the microwave and set it on the island. "You can serve this. Iced tea to drink?"

"Sure." He transferred the pasta to their plates, then sat down.

Grace retrieved the pitcher from the refrigerator and poured two glasses of iced tea. She handed one to Spencer and sat down next to him.

It was a pleasant meal. The conversation was light and didn't touch on anything too serious.

When they were finished, Grace cleared the plates. "How about coffee and dessert? Charlotte made fudge brownies."

"I've never said no to any dessert Charlotte made," Spencer said with a grin.

Grace retrieved the brownies and coffee, then retook her seat.

"Delicious," he said, sampling a brownie. "Have the police made any progress on finding whoever destroyed your lawn?"

"The captain believes there was more than one perpetrator," she replied. "He located a teenager who might have been involved, and he's hoping that with the parents' cooperation he'll find the others."

"I worry about you," Spencer admitted, "but I know you have Charlotte here and Winnie comes around often."

"There's no need to worry," Grace said. "This is my home, and I'm perfectly safe. I'm more worried about Leslie. I understand her feeling the need to leave, but it's worrisome not knowing for sure what happened. Charlotte is even more anxious than I am. She gave Leslie a cooking lesson and bonded with her, and this has her wondering if she could have helped more."

Spencer put a hand over hers. "We all make our own choices. There's nothing you or Charlotte could have done. Leslie didn't share that part of her past with you. If she had, I know you would have done anything to help her. That's who you are."

It amazed her how well he knew her.

"I should get going," Spencer said. "Thanks for a great dinner."

"Thanks for checking up on me," she said, walking him to the door. "It means a lot. Truly."

"I'll always come over." Spencer gazed into her eyes. "Whenever you need me."

"I appreciate it," Grace said. It was nice to hear.

"I'll see you later."

She closed the door after him, then went to her private quarters, where she kicked off her shoes and settled on the couch.

Winston jumped up next to her.

Grace grabbed her phone and called Jake. He was involved with a new project at work, and he told her about it in detail, his voice animated. She understood very few of the technical terms he used, but hearing his joy made her smile.

When he asked, she filled him in on their busy week at the inn. He was glad the lawn had been repaired in time for the party and asked her to update him when they found out what was going on with Leslie. She was proud of the caring and intelligent young man he had become.

After Grace hung up with Jake, she realized that she'd never finished cleaning up outside. She slipped on her shoes and headed back outside with Winston. The dog frolicked around her, chasing after squirrels, rabbits, and anything else that moved. When he ran full speed into the brush and came out sneezing, she laughed. He shook his head as if to clear it and took off running again.

She strode past the trees and flowers blooming in the late summer. The smell of honeysuckle was thick this evening. She felt as if she could almost reach out and grab a handful of it from the air.

Chuckling at her foolishness, she continued walking until she reached the site of the party. While she'd been inside talking to Jake, the caterers and the rental company had been busy. All the dishes and serving containers as well as the tables, chairs, and tent had been removed.

She picked up a plastic bag and walked around, collecting the remaining balloons and stray trash. As she worked, she couldn't help but revel in the sight of Lake Haven. It was the ideal backdrop to the McFarlands' anniversary party.

When she finished cleaning up, she called to Winston, and the dog trotted over to her. They returned to the inn and went to their bedroom.

She yawned as she checked the clock. It was still early, but she was exhausted.

As if reading her mind, Winston jumped into his dog bed and curled up.

"I guess it's been a long day for all of us," Grace remarked with a grin.

As she got into her bed, she grabbed the book on her nightstand. Reading always helped her relax.

The phone rang, startling her, and she rushed to answer.

"This is Mason. I wanted to let you know that we found Leslie."

"Oh, what a relief," Grace said. "How is she doing?"

"She's in the hospital, but she's fine," Mason assured her. "They're keeping her overnight for observation." He went on to describe what had happened.

"Please tell her that her room is waiting for her whenever she's ready to come back to it," Grace said. "Thank you for letting me know."

"I'm just glad we located her in time," he said before hanging up.

Grace immediately called Charlotte, Winnie, and Jake to tell them the good news. They were relieved and promised to keep Leslie in their prayers.

When Grace got off the phone, she breathed a sigh of relief. She was so thankful that Leslie was all right and the terrifying ordeal was finally over.

23

Jesse

Jesse stared at his father. "You really want me to work for you?"

The anniversary party was over, and Jesse and his family were sitting on the back veranda at the inn. His dad had just given Jesse the surprise of his life.

"I do," his father answered and leaned forward. "I must warn you that it's nothing glamorous. There's an opening in IT that would be perfect for you, and I would love it if you would consider it."

Jesse's dad owned a small yet successful manufacturing company. Given the technical and computer skills Jesse had picked up in the military, an IT position sounded like a good fit for him. And he'd be close to his family. It would be a great opportunity to rebuild his relationship with them.

"I don't need to consider it," Jesse said with a grin. "I'll take it."

"That's wonderful," his father said, clapping him on the back.

Zach and Marlene congratulated him.

"This calls for a celebration," Zach announced, raising his glass. "To Jesse and his new job."

They all clinked glasses.

"Will two weeks be enough time for you to move and be ready to go?" his dad asked.

"That's plenty of time," Jesse answered. "I'm sure I can get there even sooner than that."

His mother clasped Jesse's hand. "If you want to stay in your old room until you get settled, you're more than welcome." She smiled. "You're always welcome."

Jesse's heart melted as he realized what his mom was really saying. *Come home. We want you. We've missed you.*

"Your friend Becca is welcome to visit too," his mom added, a twinkle in her eyes.

"Thanks," Jesse said. He needed to talk to Becca before he left and clarify where they stood. He had to make sure she understood that he didn't want to lose whatever it was that had started to grow between them. He wanted to find out if they could make something of it.

Jesse thought she felt the same way, but he didn't want to risk leaving anything unsaid.

They all talked for a while longer until his family got up to leave and head over to their hotel rooms. Marlene was exhausted from the party, but she didn't complain.

"Thank you for such an incredible day," his mom said and hugged her three children.

Jesse walked his family to their cars. His mom embraced him so long that he was sure she was making up for eight years of lost hugs.

When she finally let him go, she touched his cheek. "It's good to have my baby back."

He grinned. "It's good to be back."

"That's right. Don't argue," his dad said. "You'll always be her baby. Even if you do tower over her and could probably lift her with one hand."

Jesse laughed.

"We'll be heading home tomorrow morning," his dad said.

"I won't be far behind you," Jesse said. "I plan on leaving tomorrow too, but I want to talk with Becca first."

"Of course," his dad said. "I like her. She seems like a very nice young woman."

"She is," Jesse agreed.

After hugging his family one more time, Jesse went inside the inn and climbed the stairs to the second floor. He went to Becca's room and knocked on her door.

A few moments later, Becca opened the door.

His heart sank when he noticed tears on her face. "Are you okay?"

"I'm fine," she replied. "I was reading, and it made me a little emotional."

"I'm sorry for showing up unannounced, but I was wondering if you'd like to go out for ice cream."

"I'm always interested in ice cream," Becca said. She opened the door wider. "Come on in. Let me make myself more presentable."

Jesse walked into the room and took a seat.

Becca picked up a brush on the dresser and dragged it through her hair, then piled her hair on top of her head in a messy bun.

"What was the point of brushing your hair if you were going to do that?" he asked with a grin.

She stuck out her tongue. "This is fashionably messy, not authentically messy."

"Oh, now I see the difference," Jesse teased.

"Come on," Becca said, playfully swatting his arm. She grabbed her car keys, and they headed downstairs to her car together.

"Let's go to Aunt Patsy's Porch," Jesse suggested. "When we were there, I noticed there was ice cream on the menu."

Soon they arrived at Aunt Patsy's. When they walked through the door, the waitress Molly smiled and waved. "Glad to see you again. Please have a seat."

Jesse ushered Becca to the same table they'd sat at last time.

Molly came over and handed them menus. "I'll be back in a jiffy to take your order." She hurried away to wait on someone else.

"I haven't had ice cream in a long time," Jesse said, perusing the menu. "I know what I'm getting."

Becca scanned the menu. "Me too."

When Molly returned, Jesse ordered a peanut butter fudge and caramel sundae, and Becca asked for a dish of raspberry sorbet.

"Coming right up," Molly said and walked away.

"Did your parents enjoy the party?" Becca asked.

"They loved it," he said. "I don't remember the last time I've seen them so happy."

When Molly dropped off the desserts, Jesse took a big bite of his sundae and nearly groaned as the sweet flavors hit his tongue. "By the way, my family thinks you're incredible. I happen to agree."

"I liked them too." Becca smiled. "It was sweet how your mom kept calling you her baby."

"I think she went overboard," he said, rolling his eyes. "I guess she was trying to make up for lost time. Dad said to go with it."

"I'm glad that your reunion went so well," Becca said, her tone more serious. "I know you were worried."

"I was blown away. It never occurred to me that they might have as many regrets as I did."

"I can't blame you for that. I'm guilty of the same thing."

He raised his eyebrows. "What do you mean?"

"I talked to my mom and sisters," Becca answered. "It turns out they didn't care about my broken engagement or my made-up fiancé. They were more concerned that I wasn't talking to them and hadn't told them where I was." Her mouth twisted with chagrin. "While they were worried about whether I was okay, all I could think about was my own embarrassment."

Jesse nodded. He could relate. "What did you tell them about your 'fiancé'?"

"I told them the truth," she said. "I explained how Grace had mailed the RSVP card by mistake. I described how we met and the plan to bring you to the wedding and introduce you as my fiancé. And I told them how I don't want to do that anymore."

Jesse hadn't expected that, and he wasn't sure how he felt about it. If Becca didn't need him, was he still going to be her guest at the wedding? He didn't mind everyone knowing the truth, but he didn't want her to leave him out of her future plans. "I admire you for being honest with them. What are you going to do now?"

"I can't keep pretending I'm working when I'm not," Becca said. "It's been fun playing hooky, but I need to go home. What about you?"

"My dad asked me to work for him at his manufacturing company," he responded. "My mom said I can stay in my old room at the house until I get my own place in the area."

"That's great," she said, smiling. "What will you be doing?"

"Working in the IT department," Jesse said.

"Sounds like a good plan."

"Yeah, it is but not because of the job. I like the idea of being employed, but I need to get to know my family again. I think living in their house might drive me crazy, but I'm willing to try it for a few months. It won't work for a lifetime. Nor do I know that I want to work with my dad forever. I think he knows that. It was more like an olive branch."

"When are you going back to Ohio?" Becca asked.

"I'm planning on tomorrow," he said.

She nodded. "I'll probably leave then too. It's time."

"When I move back to New Albany, I won't be that far away from you," Jesse said. "A few hours at the most. I'd like to see you again if you wouldn't mind, and I'm still willing to attend your cousin's wedding with you."

Becca was silent for a moment. "I appreciate your kind offer, but

I need to go to the wedding on my own." She took a deep breath. "I've really enjoyed getting to know you."

His heart fell. She was going to tell him that they had no future.

Then she gazed into his eyes and gave him yet another shock in a day full of surprises. "I think I'm falling in love with you."

Jesse beamed at her. "I think I'm falling in love with you too."

She smiled. "I believe we both need to get our lives straightened out before we can see where this goes. I can't begin a relationship based on a lie. Even if we know the truth, it would be dishonest to take you to the wedding as my fiancé, and it would start us out wrong."

"I wish I could argue with that, but I know you're right," he admitted.

"You need to make sure everything is solid with your family before you bring a girlfriend into the mix," Becca said.

"It's true," Jesse said. "By the way, my mom says you're welcome at their house anytime."

"Good to hear."

They lingered at Aunt Patsy's, knowing this would be their final evening together.

When they finally left the restaurant and walked to the car, Jesse took her hand. He held her door open for her and gave her a smart little bow.

Becca laughed as she got in and slid behind the steering wheel.

When Jesse got into the passenger seat, he reached out and grabbed her hand again. On the drive to the inn, they were silent. Not because they had nothing to say, but because their hearts were so full of all the things they wanted to say but couldn't yet.

They remained silent when they arrived at the inn and climbed the stairs to the second floor.

Jesse walked Becca to her door and smiled. "It's been a life-changing experience meeting you."

"I feel the same," she said, returning his smile. "Will you call me?" Her voice broke on the last word.

He gave her a hug. "I'll call and text you so much that you'll get sick of me."

"Never," she whispered.

Jesse gently released her, then brushed his lips against hers. He slowly backed away from her, memorizing every feature of her face to keep with him until they met again.

She cleared her throat. "Should I come downstairs to see you off in the morning?"

"I want you to, but I have to say no," Jesse answered. "If you see me off, I'm afraid that I won't leave."

"I know, but I can't see any other way to do this," Becca said. "If we're to have a positive future, I don't want ghosts from our pasts to haunt us."

Jesse nodded.

"Tomorrow when you leave, please know that I'll be out on the veranda, thinking of you and praying for a safe journey."

"Thank you," he said. "We'll see each other again soon."

It took all his willpower to walk away from her and return to his room.

Early the next morning, Jesse woke feeling refreshed. He was excited about embarking on this new stage of life. He was anxious to see his family again and begin his new job, and he couldn't wait to spend more time with Becca. He was so lucky that she was interested in getting to know him better too.

After showering and packing his duffel bag, Jesse called a taxi and went downstairs. It was tempting to stop by Becca's room one last time, but he didn't.

However, he did send her a text. *On my way.*

Becca responded immediately. *I'm on the veranda. Be safe.*

When Jesse arrived on the first floor, Grace was manning the reception desk. She greeted him with a smile as he approached the desk. "Are you checking out? Would you like to stay for breakfast? It'll be ready soon."

"No thanks," he said, setting his duffel bag on the floor. "I want to get an early start."

"I'll pack you something to eat and a cup of coffee," Grace offered. "You shouldn't travel on an empty stomach."

"I'm not hungry, but coffee would be great," Jesse said. "Thanks for everything. My parents had a wonderful time at the party. We're grateful for everything you and Charlotte did, especially for going above and beyond to make it perfect even with the attack on your lawn."

"I'm so glad," Grace said as she checked him out. "I hope you enjoyed your stay with us."

"I did. It made such a difference. I'll never forget this place."

Winston bounded into the room and yipped.

"I won't forget you either," Jesse said with a laugh. He reached down to pet the dog.

Grace left the room and soon returned with a to-go cup of coffee. "Give my regards to your family, and thanks for staying with us."

A car horn sounded outside.

"That's my ride," Jesse said. He gave Winston one last pat and picked up his duffel bag, then accepted the coffee. "Thanks again."

"Have a safe trip," Grace called.

Jesse walked out the door and descended the steps. As he tossed his duffel bag into the taxi and got in, he imagined Becca standing on the veranda and watching him.

He vowed to get his life in order and mend the relationships with his family. After that, he'd go and see Becca. And someday when their lives were settled, he'd bring her back to the Magnolia Harbor Inn.

It would be a wonderful place for a honeymoon.

24

Grace

Grace was surprised when Jesse checked out of the inn so early. After seeing him off, she hurried to her private quarters to finish getting ready for church. Grace and Charlotte took turns attending Sunday services so one of them could remain at the inn.

Before leaving, Grace stopped in the kitchen to say goodbye to Charlotte.

Her sister was frantically typing on her cell phone. She glanced up and raised one finger, asking Grace to wait.

The only person that Grace could imagine her sister texting with that much energy was Dean.

Smiling, Charlotte stopped typing, then faced her sister. "What's up?"

Grace chuckled. "Is everything okay?"

Her sister waved a hand, dismissing her concerns. "Never better."

"What does Dean have to say? Anything new and exciting?"

"We're planning our next date."

"I'm heading to church," Grace said. "How's breakfast coming along?"

"I have a casserole in the oven and a fruit salad in the fridge," Charlotte said. "Coffee and orange juice are already in the dining room."

Winston entered the kitchen and plopped down at Charlotte's feet, knowing that if he was cute enough, there was a good chance she'd sneak him something.

"I have a special treat for you too," Charlotte promised as she scratched behind his ears. "But you'll have to wait until after breakfast."

Grace laughed. "I'll see you two later."

When Grace returned to the inn after church, she saw Captain Daley's cruiser. She exited her vehicle and hurried inside, hoping he had news about the vandalism.

Charlotte and the captain were talking in the foyer.

"Sorry to barge in on you two like this," Daley said. "But I wanted to update you on the vandalism case."

"Let's talk in the living room," Grace suggested.

"I'll fetch some snacks," Charlotte offered. "Be right back."

Grace escorted the captain to the living room. He sat down on one of the chairs, and Grace took a seat on the sofa facing the window.

Charlotte bustled into the room with a tray. She gave Daley and Grace glasses of iced tea and pieces of peach cobbler, then sat down next to Grace with her own.

"Thanks," the captain said. He took a bite of the cobbler. "Wonderful as always. Anyway, I wanted to stop by to let you know that we finally managed to catch the vandals."

"So you were right that more than one person was responsible," Grace said.

"Yes, there were three of them," Daley said.

"All high school students?" Charlotte asked.

The captain nodded.

Grace took a sip of her tea. She was stunned that three local teenagers could be intent on destroying history that the town was so proud of.

"Not one of them has ever been in trouble before," the captain continued. "I don't think they'll get much by way of punishment.

Community service would be my guess. When I confronted them, two of them seemed sincerely remorseful for what they'd done."

"Hold on a moment," Grace said. "How did you find the other two?"

"Well, it was as I suspected," Daley answered. "Once the parents of the first boy found out what he had done, they were astounded and ashamed. Their son is an honor student. He has never been in any kind of trouble his entire life. Now, because of this, they were worried that his future would be destroyed. He applied for a baseball scholarship, which he might not get if he was in serious trouble with the law."

"Did he tell you who his friends were?" Charlotte asked.

"No, and I didn't expect him to," he said. "Boys don't want to snitch on each other. I know situations when the entire team or class was punished for something one person did because no one would give him up. Sometimes we never find out who did it. This time we got lucky, because the parents remembered who their son was with on the night your yard was damaged."

As badly as Grace wanted the perpetrators caught, she couldn't help but feel bad for the boy whose parents snitched for him. "School will probably be rough for the boy who lost his pin."

"No doubt," Daley said. "Still, the law needs to be followed. This is a good lesson for them all to learn."

Grace remembered something. "Was this same teenager who lost his pin involved in the other cases of vandalism?"

"No, he was only involved in the one here," the captain replied. "And all he did was act as a lookout. The same with one of the other boys. The teenager with the ATV was the one who did the real damage in all the instances."

"But why?" Charlotte asked.

"It's a sad story," he said, leaning back in his chair. "The family moved to town about three years ago. Moving is a regular occurrence for them. The kid is only seventeen, and he's already lived in eight states."

"How awful," Grace said. She couldn't imagine being moved around that much as a child.

"This is the longest he's ever stayed in one place," Daley went on. "His father is a historian, and he travels to different states to research various historical sites. He writes books and gives lectures. When he's done, his publisher tells him what they want him to research next, and within a month, the entire family is uprooted again."

"If he's been in Magnolia Harbor for three years, then he's spent almost his entire high school here," Grace remarked.

"Yes, the boy will be a senior this fall," the captain said. "A few weeks ago, his dad got the call to move to Texas. The boy asked his parents if he could stay here to complete his senior year."

"What did his parents say?" Charlotte asked.

"They argued over it," the captain said. "His mom wants them to stay so the boy can finish school, but the dad decided they're moving. He doesn't want to lose his contract. His publisher has told him that if he can't fulfill it, they'll sue him for breach of contract and find someone else who can write the books."

"What a terrible position to be in," Charlotte said. She'd recently lost her contract with her longtime publisher, so Grace guessed she knew how the boy's father felt.

"I understand the frustrating situation," Grace said. "But I don't understand why he took it out on the places he vandalized."

"He was venting." Daley shrugged. "In a way, I think he was trying to get even with his dad by vandalizing the historical places that are so important to him and his work."

Grace tapped her chin. "If he were to get community service, maybe he could help restore the places he damaged."

"He's leaving," Daley said.

"Wouldn't he have to stay in town if he was given a sentence?" Grace asked. "Or could he and his mother stay for one year and then join the father? Families do it all the time."

"It's up to his parents." The captain stood. "Thank you for the cobbler and the iced tea."

Grace and Charlotte walked him to the front door.

"Thanks for letting us know," Grace said.

"Please let me know if you have any more trouble." Daley opened the door and left.

A moment later, Winnie strolled inside. "What was the captain doing here?" She studied her nieces' faces. "Is something wrong?"

"Daley found the vandals, but it's a sad story." Grace told Winnie about what had happened.

"Oh dear." Winnie clucked her tongue. "I feel awful for the whole family."

Charlotte nodded. "I don't know their points of view, of course, but I can't imagine this is easy on any of them."

As Grace discussed the situation with her aunt and sister, she was overwhelmed with gratitude for Jake. She was so thankful that she hadn't had to face something like that when he was in high school. It had been difficult enough raising him on her own. She was proud of the teenager he'd been and the young man he was now.

"Have you heard anything else about Leslie?" Winnie asked.

"Not yet," Grace said.

"I'm so relieved that she's all right," Charlotte said.

"Me too," Grace said. "I still can't believe that her ex-boyfriend kidnapped her. What a terrifying experience."

"It's a good thing Mason was watching out for her," Charlotte said.

Grace nodded. A shiver ran up her spine when she considered what might have happened otherwise.

Leslie

When Leslie opened her eyes, she realized that she was in a hospital room. She glanced to the right and saw Mason sitting in a chair next to her bed.

"I have to go," she said, struggling to get out of bed.

"Wait." He jumped out of his chair and helped her to sit up. "You need your rest."

She blinked at him, and her head spun.

Mason held on to her. "Are you all right?"

"Yes," Leslie said. "Why am I in the hospital?"

"You went into shock yesterday after I caught up with you and Canfield," he explained. "The doctors decided to keep you overnight for observation."

She processed his words. "It's Sunday?"

Mason nodded.

Leslie let her mind drift back to the last few days. One thought stood out. "Have you been following me?"

He raised his eyebrows. "Somehow that wasn't the question I thought you'd ask. Yes, I've been following you, but it wasn't because you're in trouble."

"Then why?" she asked. "You scared me to death, popping up wherever I went."

"I apologize for that. It was my mistake," Mason admitted. "I've been following you to protect you."

"I don't understand."

"We've been watching Canfield for a long time," he said. "We were able to get a warrant to tap his phone, so we heard him tell one of his friends that he installed a tracking device on your car. When you left your house and he said he was coming after you, we used your cell phone signal to follow you. At the inn, I removed the tracking device, hoping it would give us more time to get to him before he could locate you."

"I turned my phone off before I left the inn, so how did you find me?"

"We spotted your car on the side of the road," Mason replied. "I had them replace the tire, but by then I was afraid we'd never figure out where you went. Fortunately, someone saw you apparently arguing with Canfield and recognized him from the BOLO. We were close by and able to intervene before it was too late."

"Thank you for saving my life," she said softly.

"I'm glad I could help."

Leslie was silent for a moment. Now that the nightmare was over, she was at a loss for what to do next. "I've been so focused on keeping one step ahead of him that I don't know where that leaves me."

He pursed his lips as he seemed to ponder her statement.

Leslie got the feeling there was something on his mind, but he was hesitant to say it. "Spit it out," she told him.

Mason appeared startled. Then he threw back his head and laughed.

Now that she wasn't afraid of him, she could appreciate how handsome he was.

"Why don't you return to the inn?" Mason suggested. "I told Grace what happened, and she said your room is waiting for you." He smiled. "And I would like the opportunity to escort you to dinner. We could get to know each other."

Leslie wasn't quite sure what to make of all this. The man was handsome, but as she had already learned, good looks did not equal a good person. "Where do you live in New York?" she blurted out.

"Rochester. We're less than an hour from each other."

She mulled it over. It would be nice to share a meal with the man who had saved her life. They might even become friends. She could certainly use a friend at the moment. "Yes, I'd like to have dinner with you sometime."

Mason smiled.

Something else occurred to her. "Why did you follow me? Why not just tell me what was going on? I mean, wouldn't that have been more effective?"

"It would have, but we didn't know whether you were part of his crimes," he replied. "When I was assigned to the case, there was speculation as to whether or not you were complicit in Canfield's illegal deeds. Some people believed that you had to have been aware because you were dating him."

Leslie sighed. "I've been wondering how I didn't catch on earlier. Maybe I was too trusting. Or maybe I didn't want the truth. I think I was so used to gliding through life on my parents' name and the fact that we were wealthy. This is embarrassing for me to admit, but I never even considered that I might have a career of my own before I came to Magnolia Harbor. I pretty much did whatever my parents told me to do. And after they were gone, I let Will boss me around."

"I guess that makes sense," he said. "For what it's worth, the food you helped Charlotte make for hospitality hour was incredible. I think you should seriously consider going into cooking."

"Thank you." She smiled. "That's my goal."

A nurse breezed into the room. "The doctor is releasing you in about thirty minutes. You can get ready to leave now."

"Thanks for the good news," Leslie said. After the nurse left, she regarded her hospital gown. "I can't wait to change into my own clothes."

"I almost forgot," Mason said. "I brought your backpack and purse from the car. I'll get them, and then I can drive you to the inn or wherever you want to go."

"I appreciate it," she said. "I'd like to stop at the inn and say goodbye to Grace, Charlotte, and Winnie. I also want to get the suitcase I left there."

"Sounds good. We can pick up your car on the way," he said. "If you feel up to it, maybe we can grab a bite to eat."

Mason left the room, and Leslie got ready.

Thirty minutes later, Leslie signed the release papers.

Mason ushered her to the car, then opened the passenger door and helped her inside.

When he got behind the wheel and started driving, Leslie became nervous. Mason seemed to sense her mood, and he kept the conversation light.

As her car came into view, she gasped, emotion bubbling up inside her.

Mason glanced at her. "Are you okay?"

"Yes, I'm fine," Leslie assured him. "It's hard to explain. Not having a car made me feel trapped. I missed my independence." She gave him a wry smile. "I guess that sounds silly."

"Not at all," Mason said as he pulled up beside her car. "You were faced with a horrible situation, and you needed the ability to run to save yourself. It's completely understandable that losing your car would upset you."

Leslie examined her car. One tire was obviously newer than the others. "How much do I owe you for the tire?"

"Nothing. The department will pay for it." He gave her a sheepish smile. "If I hadn't handled this so poorly, you might not have run away or gotten caught by Canfield."

"It's not your fault. He would have eventually found me anyway." She exited the car and walked to her own, then unlocked it and slid into the driver's seat.

Mason walked over to her. "Do you want to follow me?"

"Yes," Leslie said. She didn't like the feeling of someone tailing her. It was too close to the scare she'd already been through.

He jogged to his car and got inside. A moment later, he waved at her as he drove by.

Leslie followed him. As she drove, she couldn't believe how kind and considerate Mason was. Yesterday had been one of the worst days of her life, but today was a vast improvement thanks to him.

When they arrived at the inn, she parked her car. Before she had a chance to open the door, Mason opened it for her and smiled. It wasn't the fake smile that Will always used to charm people. Mason's smile was warm, and it told her that he thought she was something special.

Maybe I am, she thought. *Maybe there's more to me than I ever thought.*

Mason ushered Leslie up the porch steps and opened the front door for her, the bell above the door jingling.

As soon as they entered the inn, Winston bounded over to them and yipped.

Leslie was thrilled to see the sweet dog. She scooped him up. "I've missed you, Winston," she whispered.

Grace and Charlotte rushed into the room and hugged Leslie.

"We're glad you're safe," Grace said.

"We've been so worried about you," Charlotte added.

Leslie filled them in on the events and answered their questions.

"What a nightmare for you," Grace said. "I'm relieved it's over."

"Me too," Leslie said. She shivered.

"Would you two like something to eat?" Charlotte asked. "I can whip up something to tide you over until hospitality hour."

Leslie glanced at Mason. "No thanks. Mason and I are going out."

"Do you have any suggestions?" Mason asked.

"I'm partial to The Tidewater across the lake," Charlotte said with a grin. "Dean Bradley, the owner, is a great chef."

"And she'd say that even if she weren't dating him," Grace teased.

"Sounds good," Mason said.

Leslie nodded.

"Be sure to tell the hostess that you're our guests here," Charlotte said. "Dean will give you the VIP treatment."

"Will do," Mason said, then escorted Leslie to his car.

The drive wasn't as tense as the earlier one. Before she knew it, they were pulling into the parking lot at The Tidewater.

Inside the restaurant, the hostess warmly greeted them. "Two for dinner?" she asked, collecting a couple of menus.

Mason nodded. "Charlotte wanted us to tell you that we're guests at the Magnolia Harbor Inn."

"I'll be sure to let Dean know." The hostess smiled and led them to a table with a lovely view of Lake Haven. She passed out the menus. "Your waitress will be with you soon."

Leslie was in heaven as she perused the menu. "Everything sounds great. I don't know what I want."

"I feel the same way," Mason said.

When the waitress came back, Leslie ordered pistachio-crusted salmon and basmati rice with saffron, and Mason chose a rib eye steak and garlic mashed potatoes. They both asked for iced tea.

A few minutes later, the waitress returned with their drinks.

After she left, a tall man with dark hair stopped at their table.

"Welcome to The Tidewater. I'm Dean Bradley. I heard that you're guests at the Magnolia Harbor Inn."

Leslie nodded and told him how much she appreciated the opportunity to help Charlotte in the kitchen, along with what she'd learned. "Now I'm considering going to culinary school."

"That's terrific," Dean said, then mentioned several prestigious culinary schools with a high placement rate for their graduates.

"I'll have to check those out," Leslie said.

"Best wishes in culinary school," Dean said. "It sounds like you picked up a lot from Charlotte, so I'm confident that you have a successful career ahead of you."

Humbled, Leslie thanked him.

"It was a pleasure meeting you both," Dean said. "Enjoy your meals, and let me know if you need anything."

After Dean left to visit with the diners at the next table, Mason said, "It's impressive that people know you're going places just by talking with you."

"I never thought of that," she said. "I've been lacking in ambition for a long time. This is all new to me. I hope I don't end up disappointing people."

"You won't," he assured her. "You seem like the kind of person who follows through once you decide to do something."

"My parents always said I was stubborn."

"Stubborn isn't always a bad thing," Mason said. "Stubborn people don't give up."

Leslie grinned. Now that she had a dream, she didn't intend to stop until she achieved it.

The waitress delivered their meals, and Leslie and Mason were quiet for a few moments as they sampled the food.

"This is amazing," Leslie said.

"Mine too."

They savored their meals, even swapping bites. Now that Leslie's interest in food had been piqued, she wanted to try everything. When they were finished, they lingered over tiramisu.

Finally, it was time to go. As they walked to the car, Leslie made a decision. "I'm going to stick around a little longer. Maybe Charlotte can give me a few more cooking lessons before I start applying to schools."

"I'll be heading home tomorrow morning," Mason said. "Would it be all right if I kept in touch?"

She studied his face in the dim light of the moon. "I'd like that very much."

He smiled and shoved his hands into his pockets.

The friendship that seemed to be blossoming between them was nice. It would be interesting to see if it went anywhere. But Leslie wasn't in a hurry. She didn't need a romance in her life to feel whole.

It had taken her a long time, but she finally knew who she was and what she wanted in her life.

It was a good feeling.

26

Becca

Becca didn't know how she'd make it through Chelsea and David's wedding. Less than a week before, she had been hanging out with Jesse in South Carolina. She longed to go back to that time.

"Do you want me to help you with your hair?" her mother asked from the bedroom door.

Becca turned to her mom. She looked fabulous in an ice-blue dress. It complemented her blonde hair and light-blue eyes perfectly. Her hair was swept up in a French twist. Her mother was the picture of understated elegance.

"What should I do with it?" Becca twisted a lock of red hair around a finger and faced the mirror again. She'd opted to wear the jade-green dress she had worn to Jesse's parents' anniversary party. Staring into her reflection, it was his face she saw, his eyes deep with awe and wonder.

How she wished he were here to attend the wedding with her. Not as her mock fiancé but as the man she was closer to than any other. Her safe place and her friend.

Becca had told Jesse to stay in Ohio until he had completely made peace with his family. She couldn't regret that decision, no matter how much she missed him.

Her mother stepped up beside her. "I love this dress on you. It brings out the fire in your eyes."

"Even with my glasses?" she asked.

Her mom rested her hand on Becca's shoulder and moved closer, their faces side by side. "Glasses or no glasses, you are still my beautiful girl."

"I'm not blonde like the rest of you." Like Chelsea, with her platinum locks.

"No, but you're unique," her mom responded. "Chelsea would never be able to pull off this dress like you do. Your glasses add an air of mystery and intelligence, and your hair is gorgeous."

"Do you really think so?"

"Of course," her mother said. "In fact, I've been asked many times by my friends if your curly red hair is natural. They're jealous."

Becca was stunned. She had never heard her mother praise her looks in such glowing terms. She slid her arms around her mother's waist and rested her head on her shoulder. "I've misjudged you so much. I'm sorry."

"None of that." Her mother kissed Becca's forehead. "You and I have had our disagreements. But I have always loved you, and I have always been proud of you. I'll be better about showing you that in the future. I'm glad that you're not marrying that man today. You deserve so much better."

"I miss Dad," Becca said.

"I do too." Her mother smiled. "He would have agreed with me about David."

"I know."

They stood for a moment before Becca straightened up. "I still don't know what to do with my hair."

Her mother considered her, then said, "Leave it down."

Becca gaped at her. Her family always wore classy updos to events. It was the thing to do. "You want me to leave it down?"

She nodded. "Your hair is splendid. Don't try to hide its curls today like you usually do. It's lovely as it is."

"Thank you," Becca said. For some reason, leaving her hair down made her think of Jesse.

When her mother left, Becca took out a bold copper-red lipstick and put it on, enjoying how it brought out her hazel eyes. She also added a touch of shimmery eye shadow. She would not look like she was trying to hide. Not today.

When Becca went downstairs, her mother, sisters, and brothers-in-law were waiting for her.

Becca stared at her family, butterflies fluttering in her stomach.

They all beamed at her, giving her their silent approval.

"I don't know if I can do this," Becca whispered. She hadn't meant to say it out loud.

Veronica gave her a hug. "You can and you will. We're going to the wedding because Chelsea is part of the family, no matter what she's done."

"We're also going to show them that you are strong and not to be pitied," Victoria added. "And that David no longer has the power to hurt you."

"Actually, I've pretty much gotten over David," Becca admitted. "It's Chelsea who bothers me."

"We're not going to dwell on that," her mother said. "We can't change who Chelsea is. I would hate to see you become bitter because of it."

"I won't," Becca promised. "I will not let what she does affect me."

"Good for you." Her mom smiled. "Now let's go show them what the Hart women are made of."

The church was already filling up when they arrived.

Becca heard some people whisper and make snide comments.

Instead of hiding, she straightened and aimed her brightest smile at those who were talking about her. It might not have stopped them all, but the surprise on their faces made her confidence soar.

Veronica motioned for Becca to slide into the pew first. Becca knew the family intended to surround her in a protective cocoon.

Becca shook her head and indicated that Veronica and her husband should go first, then deliberately sat at the end of the row. She intended to make it easy for the other guests to see her and know that she was alone and fine with it.

Although her heart still yearned for Jesse.

The organist began to play, and the bridesmaids started down the aisle. All nine of them. They barely fit at the front of the church. Becca almost felt pity for Chelsea. She knew most of the bridesmaids, and she'd heard each of them saying horrible things about her cousin behind Chelsea's back. It must be lonely to have so many untrue friends.

Finally, the groom came to stand front and center.

As Becca studied David, she expected to feel something. Sorrow, anger, maybe even regret. But she felt nothing. Becca was watching her former fiancé as he prepared to marry someone else, and her heart was completely unmoved.

The joy of that moment was so huge that she grinned. He happened to glance her way and did a double take.

Becca heard some whispers. She didn't care. She was free from David's snare. He could no longer hurt her. She had suspected that she was done grieving for him, and now she was sure.

The wedding march began. She stood with the rest of the guests.

Chelsea radiated ethereal beauty as she floated down the aisle on her father's arm.

Becca realized she didn't care if Chelsea saw her. She was no longer at the wedding to prove something to her cousin. She had already proved it to herself, and that was enough for her.

Shortly after the ceremony began, someone nudged her shoulder. She looked up and gasped.

Jesse was standing beside her, motioning for her to move over. She did, and he sat down beside her.

She couldn't stop staring at him. What was he doing here? She couldn't ask without being rude while the wedding was happening, but curiosity burned inside her.

Jesse wore his dress blues uniform, and he looked very distinguished in it.

Becca noticed that he was getting quite a few interested glances. Normally, she would have felt self-conscious about the attention, but today she was so glad to see him that nothing else mattered.

Jesse might have sensed her eyes on him. He winked at her, making her heart flutter, then discreetly reached over and took her hand.

Becca squeezed his hand, letting him know silently that she was delighted to see him.

When the ceremony was over, the flock of bridesmaids and groomsmen left first.

"Do you think they have enough of them?" Jesse whispered.

Becca laughed. She had missed him so much that she couldn't even work up irritation that he had come after she'd insisted that he stay away.

Because she knew his heart. He had told her that he wouldn't come to her until he felt his past wouldn't interfere with his present. She couldn't wait to talk with him.

As the bride and groom sailed down the aisle, Becca hadn't intended to catch Chelsea's eye, but it happened anyway.

Chelsea cringed.

Becca gave her a smile, hoping it was clear in her face that she held no grudges. It was true. She didn't. Chelsea and David had stopped her from making a huge mistake, even though they had not meant to help her. Regardless, Becca had no desire to hold on to the anger and the pain that had devastated her.

With that smile, she let it all go.

When Chelsea returned her smile, Becca hoped it meant that her cousin would be happy.

They'd never be friends again like before. That was fine. Friends changed. But they would still be family.

The guests began to filter out, starting with the front row. Becca waited patiently until it was their turn.

"Are you ready to deal with the receiving line?" Jesse moved out into the aisle and waited for her to exit. He offered his arm.

She took his arm, feeling his muscles beneath his jacket. "It won't bother me. I realized that David no longer has any hold on me. I've also decided to forgive my cousin. I don't want to let bitterness steal my joy."

"You amaze me." He leaned closer. "You're exceptionally gorgeous today. Love your hair."

Becca smiled at the compliment. She would always treasure it. "I thought of you when I left it down. I don't know why."

"Because I love it that way."

When they reached the receiving line, her aunt kissed her on the cheek. "Lovely to see you. Who is this handsome young man? Is he your fiancé?"

"No, this is my friend Jesse McFarland," Becca answered.

"It's nice to meet you," her aunt said to Jesse.

Chelsea rushed over to Becca and hugged her. She truly seemed happy to see her. "I was so worried you wouldn't come. Or that you'd never forgive me."

Becca was relieved to know that Chelsea felt bad about the situation. "Did you start seeing David while he and I were engaged?" she whispered.

"Of course not," Chelsea answered. "We met again after you broke up. Everything moved fast after that. I never meant to hurt you."

"Neither did I," David said.

"It's all right," Becca said. "David, you and I were never truly suited for each other. I'm glad we learned that in time."

"Thanks for understanding," Chelsea said.

"Let me introduce you to Jesse McFarland," Becca said. "He's not my fiancé, but he is a good friend." She grinned at him. "Maybe more someday."

"Welcome," Chelsea said to Jesse. "Becca is a very special woman. If you do become something more than friends someday, I hope you'll cherish her like the treasure she is."

Jesse gazed into Becca's eyes. "I intend to."

They left the receiving line hand in hand.

"Where's the reception?" Jesse asked.

"At a banquet hall across town," Becca replied. "It's about a twenty-minute drive."

"Do you have to ride with your family, or can you come with me?" he asked.

"I can come with you," Becca said, then noticed her family marching toward them. She recognized her sisters' expressions. They were on a mission and would not be ignored. "But I think you may have to go through a trial by fire first."

27

Jesse

Jesse watched the group heading toward them and smiled. The fierceness in the expressions of the two blonde women told him that they took their roles as big sisters very seriously. He could respect that. He assumed the third woman was their mother, although she didn't look old enough to have three daughters all in their twenties.

Two men backed up the group. They walked at a more casual pace. Becca had never mentioned brothers, so they were probably her brothers-in-law. Jesse noticed that despite their casual appearance, both men were giving him a thorough examination. They seemed to be protective of Becca too.

Jesse didn't mind. That was how it should be.

Of course, Becca might not appreciate being coddled. She valued her independence. He glanced down at the woman he cared for. As he expected, she was rolling her eyes.

"Who do we have here?" one of the twins asked, narrowing her eyes.

"Yeah, who's the wedding crasher?" the other one added.

They were identical pictures of sisterly outrage.

"I told you about my friend Jesse McFarland," Becca answered. "If you recall, I did invite him."

He caught a hint of amusement in her voice and studied her family more closely. Even though they still didn't appear ready to give up their inquiry, there was no real hostility in their expressions.

Becca introduced her sisters, mother, and brothers-in-law to Jesse.

"Becca said that you two met at the inn in South Carolina,"

Veronica said to Jesse, planting her hands on her hips. "She won't tell us why you were there. In fact, she won't tell us much about you at all."

"Because some of that stuff is personal," Becca said. "Which means that I don't have the right to tell you simply because you're curious."

Jesse had to admit that he liked the way Becca took his privacy seriously. He would have been fine with her telling her family what they needed to know. But still, it was proof of how much she cared. "It's okay if you want to tell them."

The green flecks in her hazel eyes glinted. "It's none of their business yet. Besides, as wonderful as my family is, I'm an adult. I don't need their permission to invite you to a wedding." She tossed her magnificent red hair defiantly.

"You're no fun anymore," Victoria huffed. "We can't even get a rise out of you when we're being deliberately obnoxious."

Becca grinned at her. "Maybe not. But now I can irritate you by not taking the bait, and that's much more enjoyable for me."

Both twins gaped at their sister. Finally, they laughed.

"I can't believe how nasty you've become in your old age," Veronica teased.

Becca laughed. "We'll meet you at the reception. Jesse and I have some stuff we need to talk about first."

They headed to the parking lot before her family could object.

"Where can we go to talk?" Jesse asked when they were seated in his car. "Someplace we won't be disturbed."

"There's a large park near the banquet hall," Becca said. "It has a gazebo."

He started the car. "Tell me how to get there."

Becca directed him to the park.

"This is a nice area," he remarked. "It's not nearly as built up as where my parents live."

"It's developing fast. There's always a new store or restaurant opening." She pointed to an intersection ahead. There were stores and restaurants on all four corners. "A couple of years ago, those were empty lots."

When they reached the stoplight, Becca told him to turn left. "The park is down the road."

Jesse followed her directions, and a minute later, he pulled into a parking space. He stopped the car, then got out and walked around to her side and opened the door.

"Why, thank you, sir," she said, fluttering her lashes.

Being with Becca was pure joy, especially now that she wasn't carrying her heavy grief and betrayal. Jesse reached out and laced his fingers through hers, then led her to the gazebo.

"I didn't think you were going to come to the wedding," Becca said when they were seated. "In fact, I specifically remember telling you not to come."

"Well, actually, you said not to visit you until I had dealt with my issues," he reminded her. "It turned out that I didn't have as many issues as I thought."

"That's great. What happened?"

"I had forgotten all the ways my parents supported me," Jesse continued. "We talked for three hours the day I got home. I told them about Haley and my resentment during high school. My dad and I discussed our fights, and he admitted that he pushed me too hard, rather than letting me find my own way."

"Did he say why?" she asked.

"My parents were convinced that I needed a college degree to get a good job," Jesse said. "My dad wanted me to get a scholarship like Marlene and Zach so I wouldn't have to take out a huge student loan. I didn't know it at the time, but my parents were going through money problems. So my dad worried that if I got into debt, they wouldn't be able to help me."

"They wanted what was best for you."

Jesse nodded and squeezed her hand, marveling at how well she understood him already, even the things he didn't say. "He worried that I wouldn't be able to support myself when he and my mom were gone."

She leaned her head on his shoulder in silent encouragement.

"When Dad had a heart attack, my mom was so afraid that she struck out at me without thinking," he said. "She regretted it immediately, but I never came home for her to tell me. My parents have prayed every day for the past eight years that I would return to them safely."

Becca lifted her shining eyes to his. "I'm glad that you worked out these issues with your parents. And proud of you."

"Me too." Jesse bumped her shoulder. "What about you? How hard was it to come to the wedding today?"

"It was hard getting ready for it," she admitted. "But I realized I didn't care. When I saw David at the church, I felt nothing. Not even anger. I had completely gotten over him. You heard my conversation with Chelsea. She said she never meant to hurt me."

"Do you believe her?" he asked.

"I don't know, and I don't really care. That's her concern, not mine. I hope she was telling the truth for her own sake, but honestly, it no longer matters to me. I can sincerely say I hope they are happy together."

"I'm impressed."

"I never imagined I would say that. But I truly mean it. It doesn't matter what happened in the past. Chelsea and I will never have the same relationship we had when we were kids, but I can't do anything about it. Sometimes relationships change because the people in them change, and that's okay."

He nodded. "No one can alter the past, but sometimes I wish I could."

She touched his arm. "At least you were able to reconcile with your family, and you were brave enough to try."

"Speaking of family, I like yours," Jesse said. "They're protective, but I can tell they really care and want to support you."

"They do," Becca said with a smile. "The biggest surprise was my mother. I thought she was disappointed that I didn't marry a doctor, but she admitted that she never really liked David. She was only trying to be supportive. If I ever get engaged again, I hope she's honest with me about whether she likes the guy."

His palms started to sweat. Now came the important part. "I've been thinking about what you said. About how our relationship shouldn't be based on a lie. Well, it's never been like that for us. We always knew what we were doing. There were no lies told today. So right now, it seems like we have a good foundation."

"What are you saying?" she asked.

"I know we just met, and we haven't had time to figure out how we feel about each other or if our feelings will grow into something deeper." Jesse took a deep breath. "But I don't think I need more time. I know I'm falling in love with you, and I believe we have a chance to build something beautiful here."

She smiled. "I've been thinking the same thing, but I thought I was in love before. It's not something I want to decide in a hurry. I'm sorry, but I need more time."

"I understand, and I'll wait," he said. "I only recently returned and reunited with my family. I want to focus on them for now. What I would really like to ask is if you're still interested in getting to know me. My parents said that you can come and visit anytime."

She nodded. "When we're apart, we can keep in touch."

They were silent for a moment.

"I'd like to take you out on a real date before you start school again," he said. "We could have dinner, then see a movie or go bowling. Whatever you want, as long as we get to spend time together."

"I'd love that."

Jesse kissed her cheek. For now, that was enough. They wouldn't rush into a relationship. Instead, they would take it slow and steady.

In his heart, though, he truly believed that they'd become more than friends. He could very easily see Becca as the woman he'd marry one day.

Jesse and Becca arrived at the reception and found their seats at the table with her family.

Victoria glanced at Becca's left hand, then made a face, obviously disappointed.

"Sorry," Becca said. "Jesse and I haven't known each other very long. We're not getting engaged anytime soon. I'm still young. Be patient."

"That's smart," her mother said. "But then, I wouldn't expect anything less from my Becca."

Jesse and Becca held hands during dinner, laughing as they tried to eat one-handed.

Veronica pouted at her husband. "Why don't we do cute things like that anymore?"

He pretended to glare at Jesse. "Now I'm in trouble. Thanks a lot."

They laughed, and Jesse noticed that they were the liveliest table in the room by far.

After the meal, the guests started migrating to the dance floor.

"Dance with me?" Jesse asked, holding out his hand.

"Gladly," Becca said.

Jesse led her to the middle of the dance floor, and they swayed to a slow song. When the music turned upbeat, Becca's family joined them, and they all danced until they were exhausted.

Later that evening, as Jesse drove Becca back to her house, she told him about the journal Winnie had given her at the Magnolia Harbor Inn. "When I read it, I realized that if I wasn't careful, I would lose my chance at love. That's why I wanted to make sure my feelings about Chelsea and David wouldn't come between us. I didn't want to end up bitter and alone because of my mistakes."

"It was a good idea to clear up old misunderstandings first," Jesse said. "When we met today, my heart was freer than before. I have no more secrets from you, and I intend to keep it that way."

"I don't intend to keep any secrets from you either," Becca said.

"Do you think you'll be able to visit sometime?" he asked. "My parents can't wait to see you again. They really liked you."

She leaned her head back against the seat. "School's still a couple of weeks away. Why don't I come out next weekend?"

"That would be perfect," Jesse said.

When they arrived at her house, Jesse walked Becca to the door.

"Thanks for coming to the wedding," she said. "I had a wonderful time."

"I did too," he said.

"Are you sure you'll be all right driving home?" Becca asked, concern in her voice. "It's late."

"Don't worry about me," Jesse said. "I'm so happy that I don't think I could sleep even if I wanted to."

He gave her a hug and a kiss goodbye and promised to text her when he made it back.

As Jesse returned to his car, he couldn't help but smile. He couldn't remember ever feeling this content. He had so many reasons to be thankful.

He couldn't wait to see Becca again. Deep down, he knew they already had the foundation for a beautiful, lifelong love.

As for his family, Jesse was excited to return to them. It was amazing to rebuild his relationships with them and to feel their love and support.

He was so glad he'd finally decided to come home.

28

Leslie

Leslie lifted the tasting spoon to her mouth and took a sip of cream soup, closing her eyes to see if she could tell what needed to be added. She had started with a velouté base and had worried that she had forgotten one of the ingredients.

"I can't taste anything missing," she told Charlotte, her forehead creasing in concern.

"Let me try it." Charlotte plucked a clean tasting spoon out of the basket. She dipped it into the steaming pot of soup and took a taste.

Leslie drummed her fingers on her thigh as she waited for the verdict. She had learned so much from Charlotte since returning to the inn several days ago, and she knew that the chef would tell her if she needed to fix something.

"The soup is perfect." Charlotte smiled. "I wouldn't add a thing to it."

"Really?" Leslie was ecstatic. For reasons she could not understand, soup had been the biggest challenge for her. She could never seem to get the bases right. Invariably the soups were too salty, too runny, or too thick.

"I'll be sorry to see you leave," Charlotte commented. "I've really enjoyed giving you cooking lessons, and you've done remarkably well."

"I appreciate all you've taught me," Leslie said. "I can't thank you enough."

"It's been my pleasure," Charlotte said. "Have you decided what to do next?"

"I'm going to apply to several culinary arts programs," Leslie answered.

"I hope you get into the school you want," Charlotte said. "Please stay in touch and let me know how it goes."

"I will," Leslie said. "Someday I'd love to open my own restaurant, but I don't have the business expertise yet. I'd like to start out as a sous-chef."

"That's a great place to start," Charlotte said. "After I graduated from the New England Culinary Institute, I landed a job as sous-chef at Le Crabe Fou in Charleston. Then I made my way up to head chef."

"That's encouraging," Leslie said.

"And that's where I met Dean," Charlotte continued. "He took my position as sous-chef, and I was his boss for a while. We clashed for years, even after I left to open this place with Grace." She laughed. "We both thought it was a sick joke when a dating service put us together, but we worked out how to be good friends, then eventually started dating. We still compete in the kitchen, though."

"I'm glad it worked out so well," Leslie said.

"It smells wonderful in here," Winnie said as she strolled into the kitchen. She went over to Charlotte and gave her a hug.

"Leslie made a delicious cream soup," Charlotte said. "Do you want some? There's plenty."

"No thank you," Winnie said. "I've had lunch already. But I hope Leslie hasn't."

Leslie stared at her. The comment seemed strange from the hospitable Winnie. "Why?"

Winnie's hazel eyes twinkled. "If you go out front, I do believe you'll see a certain New York sergeant has arrived to visit you."

Leslie's mouth dropped open. "Mason is here? That's quite a drive."

Charlotte shooed her away. "Go on. I'll see you later."

Leslie took off her apron and hurried out the front door. Sure enough, Sergeant Mason Groves was standing there, handsome as ever.

When Mason saw her, he smiled. "I was hoping I'd catch you."

"Why are you here?" Leslie blurted out. She cringed as soon as she asked the question. It sounded rude.

Mason laughed. "My boss sent me to a specialized training. I'm going to be in South Carolina all week. He let me come down a day early to settle in. I was driving right by Magnolia Harbor, and I decided to stop in. Imagine my surprise when Winnie told me you were here too, getting cooking lessons from Charlotte."

"I'm so glad she did."

"Can I interest you in lunch?" he asked.

"I would like that," she said.

Mason escorted her to his car and opened the passenger door for her, then slid behind the wheel.

"Where are we going?" Leslie asked.

"Where would you recommend?"

She remembered the restaurant she'd visited a couple days before at Charlotte's suggestion. "Aunt Patsy's Porch is about ten minutes away. It has great Southern home cooking."

"Sounds good. I'm always willing to try a new place with two chefs' recommendations behind it."

Leslie directed Mason to the restaurant.

When they walked inside, Molly, the head waitress, greeted them. "Have a seat wherever you'd like." She smiled at Leslie. "Welcome back."

After they were seated, Molly gave them menus and took their drink orders.

Mason sniffed the air. "It smells great in here."

"The food is delicious," Leslie said. "Plus, they have the best pie for a hundred miles. The last time I was here, I sampled a few different kinds to make sure. Culinary research, you understand."

Mason grinned. "I do. How very scholarly and thorough of you."

"I'm trying to do a good service."

"I'm inspired by your dedication."

They laughed softly.

Molly returned with their glasses of iced tea. "What can I get you?"

Leslie ordered fried chicken and black-eyed peas, and Mason asked for roast beef with green beans. They both requested corn bread.

"Coming right up," Molly said, then hurried away.

"How have you been?" Mason asked, studying her. "Really?"

"I've been good, and I've learned a lot," Leslie answered. "It helped to be in a peaceful place after the situation with Will." She shuddered. She still got nightmares about being kidnapped.

"Are you having any panic attacks?" he asked. "Any ongoing symptoms?"

"Only a few bad dreams."

"So when are you going back to New York?"

"You're full of questions today," Leslie said.

"Sorry," he said. "This isn't an inquisition. I've been worried about you. In your e-mails, you've described what's going on around you but not what's going on with you."

"I've decided to apply to culinary schools," she said. "I'm also thinking about selling my house. I want to start fresh."

"I think that sounds amazing."

Leslie could tell that he wasn't judging her, and she was relieved. "The house is big and pretentious. I grew up there, but it's not home. I want a new place to make my own. Maybe a small apartment. Except I want a dog. So, it would have to be one that allows pets."

Molly delivered their meals. "Enjoy your lunch."

When the waitress was gone, Leslie and Mason started eating.

"You were right," he said. "The food is so good here."

"I'm glad you like it."

"Have you decided what kind of dog you'd like to get?" Mason asked.

"Not yet. But I've fallen in love with Winston, so I might be partial to something small and fluffy." She shrugged. "I should probably get an apartment before I get a dog."

"You don't know how long it will take to find the right place," he pointed out. "A dog would be good companionship. It could also make you feel more secure."

Leslie realized that was part of the reason she had been so reluctant to return home. Her sense of security had been compromised. If she got a dog, it might help her to feel safer. Even a small dog would hear an intruder before she would and bark to alert her. "Would you help me find a dog to adopt?"

"I'd be happy to," Mason said. "I grew up with dogs, but I don't have one now because I spend so much time working. It wouldn't be fair to the dog to be alone at my place all day and sometimes for several days at a time."

They discussed different breeds of dogs, and Mason related humorous stories about the dogs his family had owned in his youth.

After they finished their meals, they ordered cups of coffee and large slices of apple pie a la mode.

"I believe this really is the best pie in a hundred miles," Mason remarked. He leaned forward and put his elbows on the table.

Leslie immediately went on alert, her stomach clenching. A serious conversation was coming.

"I want you to know how much I enjoy your company," he said. "I realize that you've just gotten out of a bad relationship. So, I'm in no way trying to push you toward anything."

Her stomach began to unclench.

"I think we're becoming good friends," Mason continued. "I'd like to help you get settled into a new apartment and go with you to find a dog. Maybe we can go out sometimes. As friends, for now. Like I said, the last thing I want to do is rush you. But once you get your feet back under you, I think we might become something more. In time."

"What if we don't?" she asked. "What if we spend time together, and we never become more than friends?"

"I would always be honored to be your friend. I'm a cop. I get lonely, but I'm not in a hurry to marry for the sake of marriage. It would be nice to have someone to talk to on the phone after a stressful day at work. Someone to eat dinner with. Or someone to text and say I got home safely."

Leslie felt his words resonate with her. "That sounds good. I would like to be friends."

Someday she might like to be something more, but she wasn't ready to go there yet. Will had wounded her and made it difficult for her to trust anyone.

Mason might be someone she could trust with her heart. In a year or so. But not now.

When they finished their coffee and dessert, he dropped her off at the inn so he could head to his training. He didn't even try to hug her. Instead, he touched her hand and told her to be safe.

She liked that he respected her boundaries.

Later that evening, he sent her a text. *Arrived safe and sound. Sleep well. I know I will.*

Glad you're safe, she replied. *Good night.*

Leslie smiled. It was a wonderful feeling to have someone care for her like that.

The next morning, as Leslie showered and dressed for the day, she finally made the decision she'd been putting off for so long. It was time to return home. She enjoyed her stay at the Magnolia Harbor Inn, and she hoped that she would be able to hold on to the friendships she'd made here. But her life was in New York.

She wondered what her future held. Suddenly, she was excited about getting a dog, selling her house, and finding a new place to live. It would be nice to have a friend like Mason by her side. And she was looking forward to starting culinary school.

Her life would be turned upside down with all these changes, but Leslie knew that it was time to set the wheels in motion. She was ready.

It didn't take her long to pack her suitcase. When she descended the stairs, she found Grace and Winston in the foyer.

"Are you checking out?" Grace asked, glancing at Leslie's suitcase.

Leslie nodded, not trusting herself to speak.

"Let me tell Charlotte that you're leaving," Grace said. "I'll be back in a moment."

When Grace was gone, Winston bounded over to Leslie and wagged his tail.

Leslie set her suitcase on the floor. She had tears in her eyes as she squatted and petted Winston. "I'm going to miss you, boy. You don't know how much I needed you. Be good."

Winston put his paws on her knees and licked her chin.

She kissed his furry head.

Grace returned with Charlotte.

"I made cannoli this morning, and I want you to take them,"

Charlotte said, handing Leslie a container. "Don't forget to let me know how things are going for you."

Leslie accepted the container and hugged Charlotte. "Thank you for everything. You've given me a direction. I hadn't realized how stagnant my life had become."

"I enjoyed working with you," Charlotte said. "And I'm so glad that you can go home without fear."

Leslie straightened her shoulders. "Yes. Without fear."

Grace hugged Leslie and wished her well.

"Please come back again," Charlotte said.

Winston yipped as if in agreement.

Leslie picked up her suitcase and walked out the door. As she settled behind the wheel of her car, she wiped the tears from her face. She was happy and sad at the same time.

On a whim, she decided to call Mason. He probably wouldn't be able to answer, but she could leave him a message.

When she dialed his number, he picked up on the second ring.

"Oh, I thought you'd be in your training."

"I was, but we're on break," he said. "You have perfect timing."

The sound of his voice made her smile. "I was calling to let you know I'm on my way home. I just got into my car."

"Are you okay?" Mason asked.

His concern warmed her. "I did check the back seat, but I'll probably do that for a while. I'm fine. Really."

"Maybe after I get home, we can get together and make a plan for getting you a place. And a dog."

"Sounds good," Leslie said, appreciating his offer. "Give me a call when you get in."

"Will do."

They hung up with no further promises made. She didn't need

anything more. It wouldn't surprise her if something did eventually develop between them. But they were in no hurry. Leslie wasn't ready to deepen their relationship yet. She was getting stronger, more confident. And she believed deep in her soul that one day, she would be ready.

She could wait until then. Because he had promised her that he would be patient.

And Mason was a man she could trust.

29

Grace

"I'm glad that Leslie seems to be doing well," Grace remarked after their guest had checked out. She poured a cup of coffee and sat down next to her sister at the kitchen island.

"Me too," Charlotte said. "But Winston is going to miss his friend, aren't you, boy?"

Winston cocked his head, aware that he was being talked about. The bell above the front door jingled.

"I wonder who that could be," Charlotte said. "We're not expecting our new guests until later."

"I'll go find out," Grace offered. She walked to the foyer and smiled when she saw Winnie. It was always a pleasure when her aunt visited.

Winston dashed past her to greet Winnie.

"Good morning," Winnie said. Her blonde hair was pulled back, and she wore a lightweight pale-pink blouse and gray pants.

"You look lovely," Grace said, giving her a hug. "Special occasion?"

"No," Winnie said with a laugh. "I'm going to Spool & Thread and thought I'd stop by for a few minutes to say hello to my favorite nieces."

"Favorite niece? She must mean me," Charlotte teased as she came in and hugged Winnie.

"Now you behave. I said nieces, plural," Winnie gently chided. "Anyway, I was telling Grace that I'm on my way to town, but I wanted to stop by first."

"We're glad you did," Charlotte said.

"Charlotte especially," Grace said in a mock undertone. "She's in mourning. Her student checked out this morning, and I think she's going to be lost for a bit."

Charlotte swatted at her. "I am *not*. I will miss Leslie, but I'm excited for the new things in her life."

"I'm so happy that things are improving for her," Winnie said. "Especially after the trauma she went through."

"I think there's a spark of romance between her and Mason," Grace said. "It's sweet."

"Speaking of romance, have you checked the inn's e-mail yet?" Charlotte asked her sister.

Grace shook her head. "Is there something particular I should see?"

"I don't want to spoil the surprise," Charlotte answered. "But I will say there's one message that I think you will enjoy reading very much."

Intrigued, Grace moved behind the reception desk to the computer. "Hold on a second. Let me find it." There were several new inquiries. Nothing out of the ordinary there. "There's a message from Becca. I wonder how everything turned out at her cousin's wedding."

"Oh, that's right," Winnie said. "What does it say? Don't keep us in suspense."

Grace laughed. "Let me see." She scanned the e-mail. "Oh, Jesse attended the wedding with her. I'm not surprised since they seemed to be getting close while they were here. It went well. And . . ." She let her voice trail off for dramatic effect.

"And what?" Winnie asked.

"Now they're dating," Grace continued. "Becca says they're going to see where this relationship leads."

Winnie clapped. "Another romance thanks to the Magnolia Harbor Inn."

Olivia entered the foyer, somehow resplendent in a simple sundress. "How lovely," Winnie said.

"Do you think so?" Olivia twirled, showing off. "I've been waiting to wear this dress forever."

"What's the occasion?" Winnie asked.

Grace cringed at her aunt's innocent question. She didn't want to know. Other than her impromptu dinner with Spencer on Saturday after the anniversary party, she hadn't seen him. In fact, whenever his name was mentioned, it seemed he was going out on yet another outing with Olivia.

Grace had no reason to feel jealous, but she did anyway.

"I'm spending the day with Spencer. We're going sightseeing and out to lunch." Olivia leaned closer to the ladies. "Am I wearing too much perfume?"

"Not at all," Grace said. "It's an enchanting fragrance."

Spencer walked through the door.

Olivia strolled over to him, her momentary lack of confidence a thing of the past. She smiled and fluttered her eyelashes at him as he greeted her, then kissed him on the cheek.

"Good morning, ladies." Spencer smiled at Grace, Charlotte, and Winnie. Then he turned to his date. "You look fantastic as usual. Ready to go?"

Olivia nodded. With a fluttering wave, she latched onto Spencer's arm and walked out the door with him, chatting the entire time.

It was almost more than Grace could bear. She was mortified to realize that there were tears in her eyes. Blinking them back, she turned her head to avoid looking at Winnie and Charlotte.

Of course, neither woman was fooled.

"Don't let it get to you." Charlotte wrapped her arm around Grace's shoulders. "She won't be in town forever. Sooner or later, her business in Magnolia Harbor will come to an end, and she'll return to Texas. He's just being polite until then."

"You really think so?" Grace asked.

"Absolutely," Winnie assured her. "You know what we should do?"

"What?" Grace grimaced at how weak and watery her voice sounded.

"We should have a girls' night in," Winnie replied. "We can eat dinner and chocolate and watch a good movie."

"That's a great idea," Charlotte said. "I have a new recipe I've been wanting to try. You two can be my guinea pigs. It's heavy on the comfort, what with me mourning the departure of my student and all."

"I can't wait." Grace laughed in spite of her low spirits. She could always count on her family to try to cheer her up when she was down.

Even Winston seemed determined to make her feel better. He padded over to her and sat at her feet, whining and scratching at her pant leg with his paw.

Grace bent down and picked him up. Hugging him tight, she rubbed her cheek against his soft head. "Thanks. I'm blessed to have such an amazing family." She meant the words with all her heart. She knew that she could always count on her family to support her.

Her heart still ached, knowing that Spencer was seeing someone else. She couldn't do anything about that. And maybe she had lost her chance for something more with him. She would learn to be okay with that too. She had her family at her side to help her through whatever came her way.

"Instead of cooking, should we order takeout, maybe from Why Thai?" Grace asked her sister. "You've been cooking all day."

"You know how much I enjoy cooking."

"But if we get Thai food, none of us will have to do dishes," Winnie reasoned. "Plus, we'll be supporting a local business."

Charlotte laughed and shook her head. "All right. Why Thai does sound really good."

After Winnie left and Charlotte headed to the kitchen to prepare appetizers for hospitality hour, Grace went upstairs to clean the suites. As she worked, she hung on to the idea of spending time with her sister and aunt. It would be a special evening.

When Grace was finished with the rooms, she returned downstairs. The front door opened, and a young man she didn't recognize entered. He stopped in the doorway, appearing lost.

Winston burst into the room and trotted over to the young man. He reached down to pet him.

"That's Winston. He's our welcoming committee," she said, smiling. "I'm Grace Porter, one of the owners. Can I help you?"

The young man didn't return her smile. In fact, he looked a little sick. "I'm the one who messed up your lawn. I wanted to apologize and thank you for dropping the charges."

Grace nodded. "I heard that you were working to pay off the damages. I can respect owning up to your mistakes."

He shuffled his feet. "I was angry, but I had no right to damage your property. I'm sorry. I'll never do anything like that again."

"I appreciate your apology." She hoped she wasn't being naive, but she believed him. "I heard you're moving. That must be hard, especially since you'll have to leave your friends behind."

He gave her a small smile. He was a handsome young man, especially without a sullen expression. "My dad is moving for his job. My mom and I are staying here until I graduate. He'll be flying back and forth to see us every weekend."

She tilted her head and considered him. "That sounds like quite the sacrifice your parents are making so you can finish school here. They seem like good people."

"They are. My dad works really hard. Sometimes I forget how hard." He stepped back. "Well, I'd better go. I just came to say I'm sorry." He turned and almost ran out the door.

When he was gone, Grace realized that the young man hadn't mentioned his name. It didn't matter. He had owned up to his mistake and had apologized. She had certainly never expected that to happen.

Hopefully, now that he had started to make amends, he would finish his senior year without getting into any more trouble. It was hard to imagine what he must be feeling, but it did say a lot about his character that he had come here and apologized.

"Let's go get a snack," Grace told Winston.

The dog yipped and followed her through the foyer.

Halfway through the room, she paused to appreciate her lovely surroundings. Grace saw this beautiful inn every day of her life, but sometimes she took it for granted. For a moment, she reflected on the rich history that had created this majestic mansion.

The Magnolia Harbor Inn was not only the bed-and-breakfast that she enjoyed running with her sister. It was so much more than that. It was the only place in the world that she wanted to be.

It was home.

Up to this point, we've been doing all the writing. Now it's *your* turn!

Tell us what you think about this book, the characters, the plot, or anything else you'd like to share with us about this series. We can't wait to hear from *you*!

Log on to give us your feedback at:
https://www.surveymonkey.com/r/MagnoliaHarbor

Annie's FICTION